Award-winning science fiction magazine published in Scotland for the Universe

I0731234

CYMERA

SCOTLAND'S FESTIVAL OF SCIENCE FICTION, FANTASY & HORROR WRITING

ISSUE 35:
SUMMER 2023

ISSN: 2059-2590
ISBN: 978-1-7396736-9-7

Submissions of fiction, art, reviews, poetry, non-fiction are welcomed: visit the website to find out how to submit

www.shorelineofinfinity.com

Publisher
Shoreline of Infinity Publications /
The New Curiosity Shop
Edinburgh
Scotland

190523

EDITORIAL TEAM

Co-founders:
Noel Chidwick,
Mark Toner

Deputy Editor
Poetry Editor:
Russell Jones

Fiction Editor:
Eris Young

Reviews Editor:
Ann Landmann

Non-fiction Editor:
Pippa Goldschmidt

Marketing &
Publicity Editor,
Proof Reader:
Yasmin Kanaan

Production Editor:
Noel Chidwick

Copy-editors:
Pippa Goldschmidt
Russell Jones
Iain Maloney
Eris Young
Cat Hellisen
Andrew J Wilson

*This issue is dedicated to the memory of **Eric Brown**. Friend of Shoreline, great science fiction writer and all round wonderful human being. We need more Eric Browns in this world, not fewer.*

CONTENTS

COVER ART
Stref

FIRST CONTACT
www.shorelineofinfinity.com
contact@shorelineofinfinity.com
Twitter: @shoreinf
Also on Instagram

PULL UP A LOG

SF Caledonia

This is a special issue to coincide with the launch of **SF Caledonia** at Cymera Festival 2023.

SF Caledonia is a spin-off from *Shoreline of Infinity Science Fiction Magazine* and is an online magazine featuring science fiction, speculative and fantasy stories by Scottish writers. Initially we are re-publishing stories already out there to showcase our talented SF writers.

To help launch SF Caledonia, this special issue is an anthology of some of the stories and poems written by Scottish writers we've published in Shoreline of Infinity over the years. There is also a new story by Glasgow-based TH Dray to head-up the issue.

This idea came about while I was looking through the back issues. We succeeded in our aim to have a Scottish representative in every issue, and reading through, I'm impressed by the quality of the work, especially by new and upcoming Scottish writers. Scottish SF is in good hands. Where would I go to find out what else they've published? There should be a website. I aim for SF Caledonia to be that website.

Phase One begins with stories published in Shoreline of Infinity, and we're also inviting writers to submit previously published stories.

Phase Two and beyond — well, let's see how this develops.

Our aim is to establish SF Caledonia as a place to enjoy Scottish SF, past and present, and to meet the creative folk responsible for it all.

You can read more about SF Caledonia and find out how to visit it on page 100. Turn to the inside back page to find out how you can contribute.

I look forward to this new journey, and I hope you'll step along the way beside me.

And finally, a big, big thank you goes to Russell Jones, who is leaving Shoreline of Infinity to focus on his writing career. He joined us with Issue One and organised a live event to launch Shoreline of Infinity. Without him, Mark and I would have been staring blankly at our screens for ever more.

Noel Chidwick
'Guest' Editor
Editor, SF Caledonia

SENTIENT AGGRESSIVE URBAN-LITTORAL LIFEFORM

T.H. Dray

Perched **atop the highest vantage** on Craig Street, webbed feet splayed upon a rain slick roof, I survey my territory. A wide thoroughfare of mixed domiciles: four-in-a-block roughcast flats and a cluster of new builds. North, lies a T-junction leading to a busy dual carriageway. To the south; a large supermarket with deep and luscious industrial bins.

Security starlings flit and chatter in electronic bursts, warning each other of me. As well they might. They know my designation, know I am stronger than them, for I am a SEAGULL: a Sentient, Aggressive, Urban-Littoral Life-form. Patroller of the Ayr Beach sands. Punisher of those miscreants who would dare use Company deck-chairs without a permit.

I was a Lesser Black-Backed Gull, once (lesser! The insult). But humans took me; made me a machine. They reinforced the wrathful downturn of my bill; transformed my resplendent fourth winter plumage. They filled the cavity of my breast with artillery and replaced the lenses of my eyes with sight keener than a hawk's. Sight that can detect a single fallen crisp on sandy shoreline from two-hundred feet aloft.

That, apparently, was a problem. There were injuries, complaints.

The Company ordered me to lay low for a month. Forbidden to fly, or call, or posture, my rival claimed the most prestigious perch atop Pirate Pete's Adventure Playpark. Pride wounded, I flew inland, claimed this roof, this street, as my territory-in-exile.

A breeze stirs, ruffles my carbon-fibre feathers. I turn a baleful eye upon the humans below. A white-haired lady – more puffer-coat than human – walks with grim purpose towards the large supermarket. A man hangs paint-spattered overalls on a washing line. A group of children toss a football back and forth across the road. One little girl stares at me. My facial recognition software assesses her. Frizzy brown hair, dark eyes enhanced by artificial lenses, and a mouth full of metal. This is Jade Thompson, aged 10, of domicile 43a, Craig Street.

Though my threat scanners read negative, I do not like the way she stares. In a show of dominance, I spread my wings and fire my eye lasers. White hot beams score twin scorch marks across the tarmac. The man swears and drops his washing in fright. The white-haired lady shakes her head, mutters something about "phoning the council." I throw back my head and laugh raucously. As if a terse letter from a mere municipal authority could stop me!

Jade Thompson gathers up her football, waves goodbye to her friends, and retreats into her domicile, glaring at me as she closes the door.

I have prevailed, but Jade Thompson's threat status may change at any moment.

From my rooftop base, I initiate a surveillance campaign to observe her daily habits. Though her bedtime is 9pm, Jade Thompson stays up late into the night, using her phone to access a website named CrowdFunder. I do not know what this means.

One month later, a truck pulls up outside Jade Thompson's domicile. Two couriers deposit a wooden crate upon the pavement and knock the door. With suspicious alacrity, Jade Thompson answers, nods in response to questions asked by the delivery drivers, then rises on tiptoe to sign a proffered document. She retreats briefly into her domicile, reappears with sturdy scissors, and hacks at the plastic strips holding the lid in place. Before she severs the final cord, she scans the rooftops, spots me. A wicked grin stretches her round face.

Snip. The cord splits and the lid bursts open. A dark streamlined shape erupts from the crate in a thunderclap of wings. I need no recognition software to categorize that blunt head; that broad-shouldered, aerodynamic chassis; the blue-grey iridescent plumage. This is a Pinpoint Geospatial Neutraliser. A PIGEON unit.

Does this foolish little human believe a PIGEON unit could defeat me? Before humans made me a machine, I destroyed organic pigeons, seized them by their necks and shook the life from their fragile bodies. I shrieked as I tore into their gizzards, dyeing the yellow length of my bill with their blood. This interloper will share their fate.

In two heavy wingbeats, I am airborne. The PIGEON unit streaks towards me, and as we meet in the sky above domiciles 14a through d, we pause, draw back our wings and bring them down like the hammer of gods. Pressure waves collide with a boom that shakes Craig Street. Car alarms wail. Curtains twitch. A dog barks. Jade Thompson winces and covers her ears.

A fierce aerial battle rages. The PIGEON swoops and dives, dodges blasts from my laser cannons, deflects sonic shrieks that would scramble its neural networks. Humans emerge from their domiciles; stand openly on the street to gawk. Some cheer for the PIGEON unit.

Foolish humans. I will crush their joy.

The hatch on my flank opens and I deploy S.E.E.D.: my Secret Emergency Enemy Diversion. Oats, rice, crushed peanuts and delicious sunflower seeds fall and scatter upon the pavement; a most nutritious rain. The PIGEON unit emits an electronic *coo* of delight and swoops to land, to claim this unexpected prize. Jade Thompson jumps up and down, waves her arms. The

PIGEON unit heeds not her frantic warnings; is content to greedily peck at grain.

Now, I will strike.

I tuck my wings close and drop like a falcon. The assembled humans gasp. Jade Thompson shrieks, gestures at the PIGEON unit, points at me, but I have readied the armour-piercing nail of my bill.

Wind hurtles past. My wings are thunder. The PIGEON pecks, oblivious. My radar pings. Impact in eight metres, seven, six. Victory is imminent. My heart sings with glee.

At five metres, four… the PIGEON unit's blunt head turns and in the glowing red of its eyes I detect no sign of unawareness. Alarms clamour. Threat! Threat! But I am falling too far, too fast to counter.

A static burst of communication spikes through my mind. Through the soft, round-vowelled cadence of pigeon-speech, I discern three chilling words: "Engage: ROCKET BEAK."

The PIGEON unit's stumpy beak clamps shut, detaches from the fleshy white moorings of its nares with a pneumatic hiss. Somewhere in the cavity of its tiny skull, propellant ignites. *Bang!* The beak rockets towards me, slams into my bill. Electric pulses fill my head. Pain. Pain. I drop to the pavement, bounce once, twice, and land in a heap on a square of lawn. The humans of Craig Street cheer.

Lying spread-seagulled on the pavement, battered, singed, defeated, I stare wide-eyed at the sky. My life flashes before my eyes. Deckchairs, ice-cream, sand and thievery. How had my hubris led me to this end? Never before have I tasted defeat. I do not like it. It is sour and churns in my guts like hot dog onions.

<chrk> The PIGEON unit's static communication intrudes again.

"SEAGULL unit, my client wishes to speak to you."

Jade Thompson looms over me, baring her mouth full of metal in a savage grin.

"Can you hear me, Seagull?"

My throat clicks three times in acknowledgement. Weak, pathetic sounds.

"If you promise to go away and never bother us again, I'll take you in and patch you up."

Had impact not stolen all air from my lungs, I would caw in this arrogant young human's face. Patch me up? Me: the twelfth most advanced security SEAGULL on the market?

"We have Wotsits."

I pause. Wotsits. I do like Wotsits.

An alert pings. The other adult humans are approaching. Some of them look angry.

It would do no harm to concede, I suppose. Were Jade Thompson to "patch me up," I could devour her Wotsits, fly back to Ayr beach, soar over sand and sea again, resume the mantle of "Terror of the Deckchairs", and reclaim my rightful perch atop Pirate Pete's Adventure Playpark. After a Company-agreed period of time, of course.

The PIGEON unit's red eye flashes off and on. A wink.

Of course, I have no choice. But I am a SEAGULL. Our pride is boundless.

I wait a moment, regard Jade Thompson with a haughty eye, then slowly, slowly extend one white feathered wing.

T.H. Dray is a writer of speculative fiction whose short work has appeared in BFS Horizons, The Best of British Science Fiction, and was nominated for a British Fantasy Award. She is from Glasgow and still lives there in a house where humans are outnumbered by dogs.

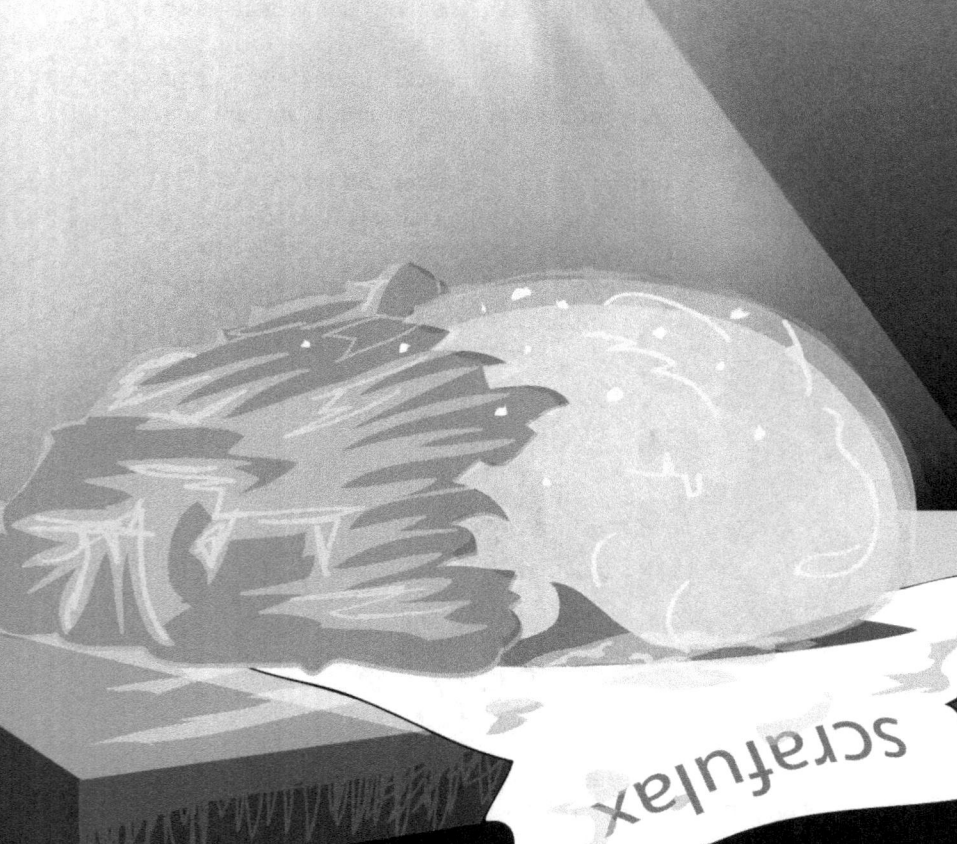

Secret Ingredients

Callum McSorley

I'm a line cook. This is how I became a spy:

I come from a binary solar system. We don't have what other beings might call day and night. Nor do we measure days like they measure days, or years like they measure years. I can't tell you how old I am, not in a way that would satisfy you. All I can say is, the first time I saw the dark – the real, deep dark – was the first time I left home. I looked out at the obsidian void from the window of the ship, and knew I was gone and never going back. Goodbye, Mama. Goodbye, Papa.

The job was waiting for me: Barkbere's Bistro. The restaurant was in an old ship which had landed by the bay, disgorging the first inhabitants of Nilvur. These were Barkbere's ancestors. I don't know how long ago this was, but it was Barkbere senior who advertised the job and Barkbere junior who was running the place when I arrived.

He was a well-dressed crustacean who lived in his office, the former captain's quarters. When we finally met, he looked at me as if he wanted to run his feelers over my skin. "A humie," he said. His throat clicked as he spoke. "I've never hired a humie before. Dad must have had his reasons."

I started to expound on my resumé, but he held up a claw for silence. I dry swallowed my words, my memorised and polished speech on craft, passion and teamwork going down like a half-chewed hunk of meat.

"A trial," he said, nodding. His eyelids flickered. With that, I was sent to the kitchen. I passed through the dining room, still carrying my backpack with all my worldly belongings inside – a second suit and a set of knives. Empty for now, it was a great, saucer-shaped room lit by glowing insects stuffed into jars that hung from the ceiling. There were seats and tables shaped to accommodate all kinds of customers. Beings travelled far to eat at Barkbere's, even from offworld.

The restaurant might have been empty, but the kitchen was already clanking and churning and howling away. I could hear it before I pushed through the swing doors. When I did, nobody looked up, nobody stopped working, nobody noticed. The closest I got to a greeting was a huge hammerhead screeching "Back!" at me as he passed carrying a tank of slithering eels, which flickered and sparked their annoyance at being sloshed around. They would be more annoyed later when they were tipped, still alive, into the fryolator.

"Excuse me," I shouted, "where is the chef?"

"Chef's right here," a voice said behind me. Chef was a vigintipede. His whites looked like bandages wrapped around his insect body. A missing limb in his top half was conspicuous. There were many rumours about how Chef came to lose that arm, from bar fights to kitchen accidents, but nobody knew the truth, probably because nobody asked him. Chef had the eyes of a murderer, but his voice, when he wasn't calling out orders, was soft and malicious, like a pillow pressed over your face. You didn't ask Chef to repeat an order, and you didn't ask Chef about his missing arm.

"I'm Grith," I said, "I'm here for the line cook job."

"Are you?"

"Yes."

"No."

"Sorry?"

"The pot wash is over here." Three arms pointed the way.

That's how I started out at Barkbere's: in the pot wash. Barkbere was right, it was a trial. Scrubbing out burnt pots with sand and steel wool is hard work, never mind scraping the dried gunk off plates stacked up way over your head. In those early days, I didn't sleep. The only food I ate was the 'family meal' – trays of whatever was going off were roasted in the pressure oven, and left out to congeal and go cold for whoever was hungry enough to eat it.

There were staff quarters in the bistro – former dorms of the colonists – in the outer carousel of the ship. I spent most of my little free time there. One night I heard a knock at the door and opened it to find Scully the broilerman outside. "You like fishing?" he asked.

"I've never tried," I said.

It was twilight, the single sun casting an orange and pink glow over everything. "Best to fish when it gets dark," Scully said. We tramped out the delivery entrance and down towards the beach. The sand was silver and smooth, and felt nearly indistinguishable from the seawater when I ran my fingers through it.

Across the bay, I could see winking lights among the trees that grew brighter as the sunlight died. "Is that the Hideaway?" I asked.

Scully answered with a single word: "Bastards."

The Hideaway was as famous as Barkbere's, maybe more so. It attracted the same intergalactic clientele, and had a similar menu of classic Nilvurian dishes tuned up to fine-dining standard. Both fished out of the same bay, staring each other out from opposite banks across the calm quicksilver expanse of the sea. The Hideaway was a common topic of conversation in the Barkbere kitchen during prep time. The cooks wished infestations on them and hatched plans to drive them out of business, or at least embarrass them. *They think they're better than us*, was the general mentality.

"Is there a boat?" I asked.

Scully, an octosapian from Orion's orbit, laughed, stripped off his whites, and waded into the water until he was up to his waist. I undressed and followed him in. The water was cold, but that wasn't what gave me discomfort. It was the prickling sensation that worried me. It felt like the burnished, grey water was eating me.

"Watch," Scully said, as the sun dropped behind the trees and the sky went fully dark. I still wasn't used to that. You can see the stars when it's dark. You look up and you see outer space. It made me dizzy.

The sea switched on, the metal sheen now glowing with ethereal turquoise light. "Bioluminescence – that's why we wait till dark to catch the fish," Scully said. My eyes were getting used to the sudden, dazzling glow of the sea, and I began to make out the shapes moving under the surface, the stripes of eerie, glowing light on the sides of the lake creatures as they darted in the water.

"How do we catch them?" I asked.

"Like so," Scully said. A tentacle lashed out into the water, causing sluggish waves that turned into a simmering churn as the tentacle wrapped itself around a flashing fish and hoisted it out. He tossed it onto a bedsheet that he'd spread out on the beach. The lights on the fish went out.

I had a shot. I waited for the shining blue stripes to stray close, and then dove in with both hands, the water splashing in my eyes and stinging. Spluttering and soaking, I came up empty. Scully laughed and I tried again. And I missed and missed and thrashed around in the water.

"You go for a swim," Scully said, "I'll tend to business." It was fun. I got my fingers around something that slipped out as if I'd clapped my hands on a stick of butter. That was the closest I got to a catch, meanwhile Scully had piled up a slithering, tangling mass of scaled bodies with fins and pincers and dead, jelly eyes. He pulled up three or four fish at a time, his tentacles moving independently of each other.

When we had enough, I helped him haul the catch back to the kitchen. My skin and hair were covered in a grey crust that peeled off in the shower. I felt grit in my teeth for days afterwards.

There were two defining moments for me that first season. The first was the stock pot incident. Back home, I could lift a big pot by myself, but on Nilvur, the gravity is stronger, a factor I forgot to account for, and sent a whole pot of crab stock crashing over the floor in a fragrant, orange wave. Scully screamed at me. June the fryer screamed at me. Krik, the hammerhead and sauce expert, swung a cleaver at my head. Chef just stared, and that was the worst. I swept the stock into the drains that ran along the foot of each station, and kept my head down for several shifts. Any time an order came through for lake-tarantula bisque, shame turned my stomach.

The second came not longer after. Having four tentacles as arms made Scully an ideal broilerman. He worked on a huge range with twelve burners, his left tentacles whipping out to shake pans and stir pots while his right ones dove into the low-boy fridges or swept the speed shelves above his head for seasonings. I was bringing him a clean pan when a jumping jack, true to its name, leapt from the roasting pan and fell between the burning rings. A tentacle went after it in a reflex motion, and Scully howled as the searing heat burned his suckers. I put the clean pan down at the station and reached in between the green flames of the gas burners, grabbing hold of the jumping jack with my bare hand. Then I put it back into the pan and strolled back to the pot wash without a word, feeling the eyes – including both of Krik's – on my back. Beings where I come from – with two suns and no night-time and no winter season – are pretty much heat-proof. The pain was minimal, but I didn't tell them that.

Not long after, I was bumped up to prep cook, and then, by the start of next season, I was a line cook, making cold starters. However, it was decided that this was a waste of my individual attributes, and I became Scully's assistant at the broiler station. Barkbere was so impressed by his first humie that he hired another to replace me in the pot wash. This one was as white as I am black, with a shock of orange hair on his head, and spots all over his face and arms. He spoke the local language with an odd accent, but often reverted to whatever it was his kind spoke whenever he was under pressure. It came out in a jagged, nasal burr that sounded something like, "Yefuk'nbas'trtyeabsylootprikyefuk'nmoovyererce…" All in all, he was a disagreeable man, but he'd been working on a nearby planet and was available at short notice.

Around this time, a media war was brewing between us and them across the bay. We were both courting tables of critics – vultures who picked and pecked at their dishes with painted beaks, and left piles of clay droppings on the floor behind them. Barkbere took to storming into the kitchen and berating us when there were fewer and fewer guests – important guests, that is, guests who mattered – to schmooze with front of house.

"We're losing," Barkbere said, the red of his carapace turning redder. "Why are we losing?"

"Scrafulax," Chef said, in his deathly quiet voice, placid as the reservoir that lures you in on a hot day only to tangle you up in the weeds hidden beneath and drown you.

Chef was right. Scrafulax was the hot thing, *the* dish you needed to be serving. Scrafulax was a mollusc found in the deep oceans of Nilvur, dredged by squids – although Scully claimed an octosapian like himself could do it too. It looked unassuming enough, a gooey, kidney-shaped white blob covered with a see-through silky membrane inside a craggy, rock-like shell. The problem was that they were poisonous. Deadly poisonous, with a kill-rate of something like one in four. And yet, the Hideaway had them on the menu. They must have found a way to make scrafulax safe. It was destroying us. The vultures stopped coming.

Barkbere took me into his office. Chef was there too. They looked like they were going to snuff me. Barkbere clicked his pincers. His feelers were trained on me. "You've been doing a great job here, Grith," he said.

"Thank you, sir."

"How are you enjoying working on the line?"

"I love it, sir, the opportunity to – "

Chef held up a couple of hands to shut me up.

"Good, that's good," Barkbere said, clacking away, "but I have another job for you. Over at the Hideaway."

"What?"

Chef held up his hands again.

"They've heard about your … special talent…" – again I felt like his feelers wanted to explore my skin – "…and want to poach you from me. We're going to let them."

There was plenty about this plan that I didn't like. It had been hard enough to prove myself to the hardcore of the Barkbere cooks, and now I'd be back to the start with a whole new crew of tyrannical maniacs who thought little of humies and even less of former Barkbere employees. Also, I wasn't lying when I told the old lobster that I was enjoying my work on the line. Sure, I had been bullied and intimidated: I spent every morning cleaning and dehorning saltwater cacti that squirted a rank-smelling oil over you if sliced wrong. Yes, I was cut and bruised and worked half to death, and the hours were still long and the shifts still manic, but I finally felt at home. I was having fun. Masochistic fun, of course, but fun all the same. And when the team were on, we were really *on*. It was like a dance, the way we moved, the way we coordinated. Me and Scully were two parts of the same cook. The food we turned out was something to be proud of, scrafulax or no scrafulax.

There were moral problems too, but…

I put on my first suit, folded my second suit, put it and my knives into my backpack, and took the water taxi across the bay. Scully suggested that I swim.

The Hideaway was a large, bowl-shaped terrace suspended from the trees. The kitchen itself was buried under the ground below the hanging basket of the dining room, and a dumbwaiter connected the two, sending up food and returning dirty dishes. The guests ascended to the open deck by much grander lifts that looked something like vintage rocket ships, the kind of deadly things humies from Sol's orbit used to build. Probably still do, judging from Barkbere's backwards dishwasher. He was from that part of the galaxy.

15

The elevator man pointed me to the kitchen entrance, which was dug into the ground. The structure of tunnels underneath was made from hard-wearing plastic, and the whole thing looked like a field kitchen that a military unit might use.

"It doesn't have to look impressive, it just has to be clean," my new chef said. He was a big Jacintha slug called Ruis who was always smiling. He was waiting for me inside the tunnel. "You're Barkbere's fireproof humie, right?" he said, laughing. I noticed a pale stick of a being hovering around behind him with a wide mop.

"Pleased to meet you," I said. "I'm Grith."

"Well, Grith, before I show you to your quarters, there's something I want you to do – this way." Chef Ruis turned his huge body and slid down the tunnel. I realised then what the mop man was for.

We entered a utilitarian and spotless kitchen.

"Everyone listen up," Ruis's voice boomed. Many eyes turned to us, although pincers, fingers and tentacles continued to work. "This is Grith, our new line cook." He handed me a blowtorch and gently pushed me forward.

I waved at them, then, keeping my hand aloft, brought the searing flame of the blowtorch up to meet it, smiling all the while. For a second, they stopped working, just for a second, then they cheered...

...and went back to work. I joined them. It was different here. There was no shouting, no cajoling, no threatening. Even in the thick of a four-hundred-cover night, there was calm in the Hideaway kitchen as Ruis called out the orders in his cheerful boom.

I worked alongside a polite broilerman called Twitch – the title just a formality since his race are hermaphrodites – and although they only had two hands, they worked as if they had four. Twitch was covered in a fine, slick fur, wore a kind of netting rather than whites, and had a rare elegance compared to the brutes and briny cranks I'd been working with.

"Watch and jump in when you can," Twitch said on my

first shift. "That trick of yours will come in handy." During prep, they drew my attention to a voice-activated projector attached to the extractor hood, which cast out a recipe when given the name of a dish. I was familiar with a lot of them – glazed boater with mashed fatroots and truffles, griddled jumping jack and popping grain, fried saddle of elka, slow-cooked rockfruit – but there were slight differences to the way things were done. One dish involved capturing the fragrance of the stinking cactus oil, and serving it in a fog that wafted over the dining table. Apparently the vultures loved it.

At the end of a shift, I was sweating, breathless and glowing, but with nowhere to direct my energy. The cooks were happy with a shift well done and cleaned up to go. There was none of the high-spirited, wine-enabled messing around when Chef left that marked Barkbere's. It struck me that nobody mentioned Barkbere's, not even to me. They didn't think that they were better than us, they just didn't think about us at all.

I didn't say any of this to Barkbere or Chef when I made my first report. The three of us were crammed into the back of a delivery truck parked some distance from the coast, knees too close together, Barkbere's feelers in touching range, Chef's eyes lasering through me. There wasn't much to report. I'd seen orders of scrafulax go out, but all I knew was how it was plated – three half-shells on a plain board with a pile of grey salt from the bay on the side. Chef snorted and said nothing, arms and legs folded, except for the one without a counterpart. I'd tried looking scrafulax up in the recipe projector, but I was rarely alone in the kitchen and had to keep switching it to something else.

My other task was more successful. I borrowed the keys for the delivery entrance and the walk-in fridge from Ruis under the pretext of doing a stock check, and while I was hidden in the depths of the walk-in, I took moulds of them to give to Barkbere.

I decided to ask Twitch about scrafulax. "Dangerous, isn't it?" was my opening gambit.

"Is it?" Twitch replied with a smile.

"I heard it was poisonous."

"Salt is poisonous to a slug," they said.

I dropped it; I was too busy to talk anyway. The orders poured in and I stacked them up in my head, which was full of cooking times and a triaged to-do list. Arms, fingers, legs, tentacles and pincers moved and clicked like the parts of some great machine. Clean, efficient, elegant, we turned out the next dish and the next one, and the next. Communication was done in single words, clear and succinct over the kitchen noise, but never yelled. The kitchen and the restaurant were joined by more than just the umbilicus that took the finished dishes up to the diners. The atmosphere and attitude carried from one place to the other, from the ground to the sky and back.

Grassing to Barkbere was making me ill. I'd return to the restaurant from these meetings unable to look at anybody. Nevertheless, I continued to do my best to uncover the scrafulax secret. I helped the porter unpack deliveries of the rocky shells, and pumped him for anything he knew, which was little. I expressed interest in them to Chef Ruis: "I've never eaten one before, I heard they were really poisonous." I wheedled Twitch some more, and the other cooks too, and even the stick-like mop man, when he wasn't trailing behind Ruis.

After another fruitless clandestine meeting – Chef was seething, although he said nothing, as usual – Barkbere growled, "Scully misses you. He's looking forward to you coming back." *Coming back.* Was I really coming back? What for? As if I'd said this aloud, Barkbere added: "Chef needs a new underboss. The position is open, for now."

I went back to the Hideaway in a foul mood. My insides were churning. Underboss ... that was the fast track to becoming a chef. But studying under that whispering psycho, could I manage that? I did miss Scully. I missed going fishing. But working on the line of the Hideaway was satisfying in a wholly different way, if I could bring that back with me ... but I knew this wasn't possible. I was sick of the darkness – I woke up and it was dark, I worked in the false light of the kitchen all day, and when I was done, it was dark again. *How do beings live like this?*

I was making myself queasy, stirring all this inside my head, when Ruis called me over. "Hey, fireman, come here a minute, I've got something for you!" In the palm of his hand was a scrafulax, opened up, the organ gently beating inside its skin. "Tried one of these before?"

I shook my head and tried not to show how tense I was. "Is it safe?"

Ruis took the lid off a tub containing a fine, colourless powder and sprinkled it over the top. The flecks sat on the surface of the membrane then melted in. "It is now," he said, and handed it over. "Go on."

"What did you put on it?"

"My 'special dust'." He smiled. "Down in one."

I was scared of it. I looked up at the slug's smiling face and swallowed the scrafulax. It was tangy, salty, bitter. I gagged and swallowed a second time, forcing it down my throat. I felt it move in there and I choked again, my eyes watering. Ruis clapped me on the back. "Awful, aren't they?" He was laughing.

I didn't go to sleep after service. I lay awake in bed. When the noise from the bar had died, I got up, put on my suit, and bundled my second suit and knives into my backpack. Outside, it was dark again. I could see space yawning above my head, and saw the twinkle of stars millions of light years away. Goodbye, Mama. Goodbye, Papa.

I let myself into the kitchen using the set of keys that Barkbere had fabbed for me, and took a box of scrafulax from the fridge and the tub of Ruis's 'special dust'. Then I walked all the way round the coast to Barkbere's Bistro.

Barkbere woke the whole crew when I showed up. We assembled in the kitchen. Chef pried open the scrafulax and set them on the pass. I handed over the tub.

"What is it?" he whispered.

"I don't know. He called it his 'special dust'."

The vigintipede looked like he wanted to slap me with several hands at once. "Special dust?"

"It works," I said. "I've already tried it."

"How much?"

"Just a pinch."

Chef prepared them and handed them out. We stood in a loose circle: me, Barkbere, Chef, Scully, Krik, June and the other line cooks. Even the red-headed humie dishwasher was there. Barkbere obviously felt he needed to say a few words, but all he managed was, "To the future of Barkbere's Bistro!"

We swallowed them. There was a lot of choking and hacking. Even Chef couldn't keep the disgust from his face. I was prepared, and forced mine down in one great gulp, my teeth together and mouth clamped shut, an awful taste on my tongue and a strangling sensation in my throat.

"Delicious!" Barkbere cried. His beady, flickering eyes were watering, his feelers twitching in distress. "Delicious!" He clapped me on the back with one of his great claws. "You've done it, lad, you've –"

The dishwasher vomited on the ground.

"Really," Barkbere started, "that's a terrible waste, that is one of Nilvur's, if not the galaxy's, finest delicacies and..." He trailed off as the pale, spotted humie continued to vomit and grow even paler. He heaved until blood came up and then collapsed on the floor in a pile of his own viscera.

"Is this some kind of humie thing?" Krik suggested, just before he began to puke.

"What have you done?" Chef asked. He was reaching for a knife before he too dropped, holding his guts. Barkbere was next.

The remaining cooks were looking at each other, stricken with horror. I started to back away before any of them had the sense to pick up where Chef left off. Scully was watching me. He was still standing.

"I'm sorry," I said. "I didn't mean for this to happen." Then I turned and ran.

I had only the clothes on my back when I arrived at the Hideaway.

My suit was splashed with blood and bile. The look on Scully's face had followed me all the way. What had happened? Why hadn't the dust worked? My stomach was doing flip-flops, but it didn't have anything to do with the scrafulax.

Ruis was waiting for me. "You're back!" he said, jovial as ever. "How was the tasting session?" His eyes winked at the blood on my shoes.

"What happened? What did you do?"

"Nothing at all. Scrafulax is lethal in about one in four cases. I thought you knew that."

"But the dust … the special dust." I realised then how truly lame that sounded.

"Ground lice pepper. Just for flavour."

"But – but you serve it here!"

"You want to know the real secret of scrafulax, kid? The real reason beings flock to the Hideaway to try it? The risk. The thrill of it. One in four – d'you like those odds? You've eaten two already – you should be a gambling man, you've got the luck."

"Customers die here?"

"It happens, yeah, but it keeps the vultures coming back. Anyway, Barkbere's might be closed for a bit while they restaff—"

"Barkbere is dead."

"He has sons. As I was saying, you're a good line cook – Twitch agrees – and I could use you here, if you still want the job?"

I looked up at the sky: open space above the treetops, no suns, just darkness and those far-off white pinpricks that might mean life or might mean nothing at all. It was a long way home.

"I'll take it," I said.

Callum McSorley is a writer based in Glasgow. His short stories have appeared in *Gutter, New Writing Scotland*, and *Shoreline of Infinity*. His debut novel *Squeaky Clean* is out now from Pushkin Press. @CallumMcsorley

Oh Baby Teeth Johnny With Your Radiant Grin, Let's Unroll on Moonlight and Gin

Cat Hellisen

It doesn't matter how this begins.

I've had three glasses of what passes for gin in Eight to the Bar, and something that the bartender called rum but tasted like motor oil and gunpowder. I'm not drunk. I'm just talking out loud to myself.

It doesn't matter how many times you've died and died and died again, and rolled and rolled and rerolled yourself together.

Once, and once, if you're asking. I'm not one of those who hate the way I remembered myself and walk back out into the inbetween and let myself be wiped out so I can start over.

"Why not?" asks the woman. She's been here for a while, I think, balanced on the edge of her barstool, the stem of her Martini glass plucked between pale fingers. She raises the glass. Lowers it. Never drinks. She has eyes like the moon. I don't mean that poetically. I mean she has bits of dusty grey rock for eyes and she weeps silver light. Her tears leave fluorescent puddles on the wooden bar counter, and turn her drink bright acid absinthe.

Fay-juice.

She's not one of them, though. Too human looking, despite her moon eyes and her pallid skin and her coterie of satellite sisters who are ranged about her like she's a queen and they're her bodyguards. If she was Fay, she'd be prettier. Perfect. She would hurt to look at. She would laugh while she ate me.

Or if I was really unlucky, she would give me a job.

I blink, swivel so that my gun arm points lazily in her direction, and show her my teeth. Bullet cases, silver and bright.

She doesn't react.

"I invite you to this conversation?" I sneer at her, but she merely cocks her head and pretends to sip at her tear-filled drink.

"You're not having a conversation. You're sitting alone."

The bar is packed. I'm not here alone. I just have a lot of space around me. Even in the busiest drinking holes in New Hope, filled with sinners and screamers of every tab and type, few people choose to sit next to a gunman. Suicide is a pastime, but murder is a sin – you don't wipe someone out again if they like who they are. But even memories and dreams need to eat, and the Fay pay me well enough.

They used to, anyway. That's why I'm here, trying to get drunk as a feeb on these abominations that pass for alcoholic beverages. I got a job, and I turned it down.

The Fay hate that.

The woman shifts closer to me, sliding her drink along the counter and ignoring my right arm that hangs between us in warning. My gun arm is easily three times the size of my left, machine sweet, gears and cogs and sights and so hard and shiny.

"So tell me what's so great about you that you don't wanna reroll yourself." Her fingers play with the folds of my loose silk scarf, pale digits slipping into pale folds, tugging lightly.

"Everything." All of us Divers Peoples have come back from the dead, wrapped around memories and fears and loves. We are the sums of our incomplete nightmares and dreams, shaped to fit a world that no longer exists. I came back with a gun arm and bullet teeth. I shoot other people for a living. It's better than being dead. Or jackal-headed like the group of men in the far corner, or made of starlight and hunger, squat and armless. I once killed a saint who was a beehive, his mouth full of honey and his head humming with revolution.

I'm not like them. I'm safe. I was born with a weapon. Nothing can get me.

"I wish I could change," the woman says, and sighs wistfully. "Just… walk out there." She stops playing with the silk of my scarf, and waves one hand at the packed room, but I know she means the inbetween, that dimension full of human memory and soulstuff and ash and misery. The remains of the human race. "I want to walk out there and unravel."

She downs her drink and shudders.

"So why don't you?"

Head bowed, she traces patterns in the mess of luminescent tears on the scarred wood. They drip from her lashes, run down her cheeks. She's a weeping Madonna, leaving trails of light wherever she goes. "Scared, I guess."

It's not a surprise. The dead gods know what she might come back as. Right now she has it pretty sweet – she looks mostly human, even if she's grey and drippy.

"You might not even come back at all," I point out. The storms in the inbetween are constant. I've been close to the edges of the world, travelled through it. Happens in my line of work. "I've seen people march out, marched out. Sometimes they come back. Most times… well, if they do, I wasn't around to see it."

She snaps her fingers and the barman hurries over, simian face blanched under the too bright lighting. He pours us both new drinks, and no mention is made of cred. My new friend must be loaded. "What's your name, stranger?" She raises her glass in mock salute.

I should lie. I just turned down a hunt, because no damn way will I shoot a Muse, and the Fay could make life incredibly unpleasant for me from here on out. That cred balance that looks okay now is gonna look less so in the morning when I'm sober. But they'll find me, no matter what. They'll send one of the others after me if they want me dead, and no name changes will save me from that.

It's not even my real name, as far as I know. Just one that rolled up in my head like a line in a song that won't leave you. "John." Or Johnno, or Johnny, or Oh-shit, depending on how we meet.

"I could tell you that my name is Celeste," she says. "Or Selene. Or Luna."

"It's not."

"No." She stirs her drink with a tiny rainbow stick made of sugar. "It's Valentina. Drink up, Johnny-boy, we have to leave." She doesn't tell me why, but I find myself following her orders, downing my not-gin and walking out with her into the night. Her sisters have gone, melted away, if they ever even existed.

"Where are we going?" I ask her. I know New Hope well enough, though I wasn't rolled here. Unlike most of the Divers Peoples, I've travelled from city-node to city-node, tracking quarry through the inbetween. I had the protection of the Fay then, and nothing could unroll me. With a shudder, I realise that my protection is gone. Unless I'm ready to take my chances, I'm stuck in this forsaken hell hole.

New Hope. The city of endless night, haven to sinheads and screamers and every vice known to mankind in all its variations. A Court City; a life-support system for an alien race. I suppose there are worse places to be trapped.

Valentina is a moth following starlight, her cold hand in my one warm one, the weight of my gun arm slowing us as we navigate the silent alleyways. Above us New Hope's moons shimmer and shadow through the roiling clouds, boring down with the light from non-existent suns. Her lightning towers catch the storms and her edges crackle.

There are folks who live off danger. You could say, people like me, who go hunting through the inbetween to put a baby tooth bullet in the back of some feeb's head, or the sinheads on their tabs, screaming themselves into an accelerated madness. But we're the normal ones.

Other people come crawling right up to the palaces and cast anchors at the foot of their hum and panic. Hand in hand, with Valentina, I'm one of them, feeling the fear quicken through my skin and metal, a shiver of livewire dread. And that feeling, it's cherry, it's the dust from the angels on 42nd, or the taste of killing. It's sick and happy, a badgood pit-of-your-stomach flip.

Valentina takes me to a little building, grey and faceless, the pitted concrete slick with water and mould, the neon sign a pink nonsense scrawl against the flickering darkness. Company of Fools. She opens a door onto a den. Not dust or whatever, sugarsweet and sickly, but something new and strange. The place is packed but tiny, so perhaps there are only a handful of people. The mirrors and lights and curtains and veils and trails of smoke and incense stink make the number impossible to hold. Five or fifteen or fifty.

The Company of Fools is a little piece of inbetween. Not really, of course, but a small safe space where people suckle the ash of memories until their heads sing and they think they're unrolling at the edges. Not for real. Never for real. Like sleeping was to death – full of dreams and darkness, but you always woke up.

After a while I leave the fools to their little deaths and head back to safer ground, far away from Fay palaces. I need cred. I need a place to stay, food to eat, gin to drink, and for all that I need work. Only, who in their right mind is going to give me a job? Legit work, not hunting.

My options are limited. I've got one hand, which makes me slow and unsuitable for manual labour. I have a radiant grin, bullet teeth, black suit and tails, a white scarf promise. I look like I'm ready to kill anyone I meet, which is often true, and the only work I've ever done involves my gun arm. Protection services, strong-arming, something along those lines.

Perhaps I can apologise for not taking the Muse job. New Hope is a city of second chances, after all. And third and fourth and trillion. Head addled from the gin and the wretched aftertaste of ash, I trace a path through the thinning crowds back to the club where I first saw the Muse.

✳

I'm not usually one for the thunder and pulse of the Collective's hypnodance sets, but the factory-club is a routine pick-up point. I was there for cred on some mundane contract, a little baby tooth bullet to the head for some undesirable. The Collective was seething with a glitter of starshine and filth, and even I found myself trapped in the melody and spin, my heart aching, my gun arm screaming. There's only one thing that can affect the Divers Peoples like that.

A Muse.

It was on stage, The Collective dj's jacked into it, channelling beats and melodies, making the crowd shudder and surge.

Coincidence.

There's something about a Muse that makes living worthwhile. In all this mess of After, they are the only things left that are truly real. Humans, not Divers Peoples. No Muse has ever had to roll itself together out of the shreds of memory and ash. People pay good money to jack into a Muse and download inspiration and imagination, but that's not something I've ever needed or could afford.

I only need Muses to exist because they make me hope.

In that seething crowd, the music storming through the crowd and bowing them like reeds, bass vibrating through the soles of my two tone wingtips, I stood at the centre of an empty circle, smiling my bullet smile.

Mid song, the Muse looked up at me, and I could see nakedness and light inside its eyes. Truth and time, miracles and myths. I fell into its world – my world – and for one moment I was alive, my hands red-stained, gathering my mother's broken bones. The shock of the real. It hurt too much to keep eye contact and I left the club to go kill someone, to let the smell of blood and shit wash away the memory of the Muse and the promises in its eyes.

Two nights later, Frederik came to me and told me someone stole the Muse, and The Collective will be paying for us to retrieve it and the thief. Sounded fine. Except it wasn't just The Collective credrolling us our trills, but the Fay. They wanted their pet human back, and maybe I was only meant to be a bit of muscle, but I'm not stupid. Bringing a run-away Muse to the Fay was a slow and painful death sentence. They'd eat the poor fuck alive and make it love them for it.

I said I'd think about it. That's as close to a no I could give. Next morning the rest of the hunters were gone, and the Fay sent me a little present. A tin box, rusted on the edges and filled with baby teeth. I recognised it. Or I thought I did. My mother, pretending to be the tooth fairy, had kept all my milk teeth, each one exchanged for a shiny coin. I'd found them in a drawer after she died. This tin full of teeth. A rattle of protection charms, keeping me safe. No protection charms for her though, shot in the face during a break-in. Dead because she was in her own house at the wrong time.

Memories are best drowned.

The club looks derelict in the not-light of not-morning, and I'm still dizzy with fatigue and soulstuff traces. Even though the streets are deserted, nothing but rain and debris, feathers and sequins and shit, I'm certain something is watching me. My back itches, and sweat gathers in slow trickles down my skin. They will come for me sooner or later, and when they do, I'm fucked.

The Muse is gone, and I have nowhere to go. I'll need cred, and fast, if I want to make a run for it. I wonder if there's any point. Maybe I should just enjoy the last days I have left. With my true hand deep in my pocket, fingers clenched around my tin full of teeth, I trawl the bars of New Hope, getting drunker and drunker, waiting for my death to step out of the shadows.

When the darkness deepens, I head back to Eight to the Bar, hoping to catch a glimpse of the moon one last time.

All seven of the lunar woman are crammed onto the stage in the corner, their voices choiring and shimmering through the garlanded rafters, setting the glass spheres to singing. They sway and croon, arms around each other's waists as they face the rumpled audience. A poster on one pillar proclaims the act to be The Seven Sisters, and shows the moon-eyed girls in simple pen lines, haloed by bright lines of light. Moonlight spills from their faces, their endless tears spattering their grey dresses and the dog-end littered floor.

I fist the tin full of teeth tighter, the rust flaking into the creases of my fingers. Sitting at the bar, my fake gin waiting, I watch and listen.

Afterwards she heads toward me as though she's scented gun oil and baby teeth, gum rot, fire powder. "Thought you'd come back," she says as she slips onto the empty stool.

"Nice music," I say. "I remember those songs." And I do, vaguely. They were old as wars back before the world ended, oh johnny oh johnny, heavens above.

"Most don't." She takes my untouched gin and nips it. "People think we've hired a Muse."

"People are idiots."

"But you're not?"

The tin edges are scraping my hand raw. "Oh no, Valentina. I'm the biggest dumbfuck feeb of the lot." I should have just taken the job. Who cares what the Fay do to some wayward Muse and the fool who took it. "Turned down a cushy gig," I say, and run my tongue along the inside of my bullet casings, tasting the fear caught between them, salt and steel.

She takes a lace-trimmed handkerchief from her skirt pockets and dabs the light from her face. "You must have had your reasons. Some gigs aren't worth the rum."

There's no point in explaining to her that the kind of people who employ me aren't gonna worry about a bum note or a bad crowd. They take things personal. And personal, in gunman terms, is not a good thing for no one.

"Don't let this vex you," Valentina says. "I could offer you a job." She grins and her teeth are opalescent stars. For a moment, I'm blinded, brainless. She puts one long-fingered hand over mine, and her skin is cold and chalky-smooth as polished sandstone. "We can't talk here. Meet me at the Fools." Her sisters are sidling toward us through the crowd of music-lovers and moon-lovers, their faces set in celestial disapproval. Valentina lets go my hand and blows me a kiss goodbye.

✳

There's no point in staying for the Satellite Sisters' second set, and I walk out into the sweat-drenched night, the moon-women's vocals following me in silver chimes, exhorting me to straighten up and fly right. I know where Valentina wants me to meet her. The night before, Valentina led me through the city, past the haunts I thought I knew well, and through the maze of winding streets, the smoky speakeasies, the neon bars, the noodle stalls and java carts, until I'd found myself in a part of the city I'd never bothered to tread before.

The endless rain tends to rot everything in the city eventually, and the bridges that spin and span the city, the lightning towers that ring the borders, can make New Hope seem a nightmare churning of constant chaos and decay, but there are places where the ground tricks you and the sinheads and screamer packs thin out. The centre, close to where the Fay have a palace. It's not a place smart people go.

I heard a theory once how the palaces are extensions of the Fay Ships, visible only in this dimension. It makes as much sense as any of the other rubbish drunk fools spout as they wind their philosophies up around them like cloaks. And it explains why the world, which is strange enough already, gets weirder near the palaces. The world eddies, it shifts and loses focus, and Divers Peoples slip further from where they began. No one likes to be close to the palaces.

And no one wants to get eaten, not at first.

That's where Valentina would want to meet me later, in her room full of ashhearts and soft water-pipes, where the dreamers unrolled, while outside the city of New Hope stood against the storm, expanding itself memory by memory like a coral reef.

Before last night I'd never believed ashdens really existed. After all, I'd been out there. For real. Walked through the inbetween, or ridden in a traveller's carriage, and I wanted to unroll about as much as I wanted to be eaten by Fay. But Valentina was missing something important. Not her eyes; that was hardly what mattered. Some hidden part of her that made her hollow and incomplete as a doll that's had its batteries pulled out the back.

Did I want to go to her and her offer of a job?

I pause in the narrow alley. It's cold and dark and quiet. The rain falls in a soft haze, a brief respite from the storm, and all around me the street sizzles softly with water. There are no people out. They are locked up in their dens, or hidden away behind glass and stone. Underfoot, the ground pulses, steady, magnetic. A sure indication that I'm near the palace. I can even see it, a little, through the veiling rain, flickering in and out of existence, a twisting spider turning itself inside out and back again. It gives me the cold sweats, that knowledge that at any moment something is going to come up behind you and tear right through your back, pull out your insides and laugh at you as you die. I swallow. The fizz of rain masks out any other noise, but I swear I hear a pitterpatterpausepatter that sets the hair on my neck to stand up like I'm one of those fuckers that rolled together only half-human.

The Fay want me dead, and here I am, right in the middle of their web, because the only feeb stupid enough to be out here so close to a palace this night is me. Valentina is the set-up. There's no job, no rum-money, no secret trills waiting to land in my cred balance.

A high-pitched sound; a child's laugh and fox's scream that got tangled up in each other and forgot which was which. Right at my back and far away. The palace shifts the dimensions around it, pulling the silk threads of past and present and space and memory. My time is up.

The movement happens without thought. One minute I have my back to the Fay, frozecold with the knowledge that it's going to eat me oh fuck eat me oh johnny oh johnny how you can scream and the next I'm facing it, my gun arm raised, baby teeth bullets chattering through the night rain, tearing into skin and bone, spraying blood across the darkness.

It stares at me as it dies. Eyes wide, as though I've made some kind of faux pas. Like it can't believe what had happened.

Not a Fay.

Just some bonethin kid with his rows of startled eyes. Eight, all unblinking, filled with slow-moving stars, his extra head hanging small and limp against his left shoulder. It takes longer to die. "Why?" it asks in a voice too deep for its babyface, but that's all it manages before the kid crumples.

Rain mists around us, and I lower my gun arm.

Black water, the faint scent of blood, the final echo of gunshot, and then there is nothing but this body in the endless rain, and me. And no fucking Fay whatsoever.

A faint trace of smoke reaches my mouth, and I taste old blood and burned sugar before the rain washes it all away. The kid sprawls at a weird angle, body twisted, one face wrenched toward the hidden moons and the bitter sky. Lightning cracks in the distance, and in the blackwhite light I see my mother's face superimposed. A ghosting thing, quick as a wink from an angel. The other head, small and soft-skulled, stays as it is, mouth and eyes still open in accusation.

Why?

The fingers on my good hand tremble, and I tuck them deep in my pocket, folding the tin of teeth in my palm. No one saw me shoot down some stupid innocent kid. No one saw the thieves who shot my mother in the face and left the world darker and emptier.

My throat is dry, and I open my mouth to swallow the endless rain. My mother was murdered, and my memories of her made me a murderer. The teeth are a warning that my time is up and the only person who has taken the time to talk to me like I was real is some weeping singer who can't see what I am. All she wants to do is die. Not even die. She wants to be erased.

That body in the rain isn't going anywhere, and soon enough someone is gonna find it and find the baby teeth bullets chewed into its meat, and someone is going to come for me. In New Hope Fay contracted murder is fine – suicide by unrolling is fine – but even on the edges of humanity we have our rules about killing innocents.

I need to get out of here.

✳

Four thousand heartbeats pass, slow and jerky. I'm alone in the Company of Fools, curled up in a corner, my gun arm pressed against the wall as though I could will it into shadows and nothing, fall into the maze of wallpapered crimson hibiscus and grinning archaeopteryx. Perhaps whoever imagined this place into existence read the same books I did as a child, our fingers skimming the same painted illustrations of terrible lizards, the ancestors of chickens, tiny things that would become horses, rats, people.

My good hand reaches out and traces the finger-clawed wings, the reptilian teeth. It's faintly soothing, the dry wallpaper under my finger tips bringing me back to reality. Anchored, I don't do any of the drug while I wait, but ash is in the air, and with every breath my head gets fuzzier, less my own. I remember snippets of conversations I never had, I mumble to myself about places which no longer exist, and laugh with someone else's voice.

Valentina sinks next to me on the small tapestried couch. She takes a proffered water-pipe and breathes in the memories and ashes of dead human, their soulstuff filtered and sweetened to taste. She drips moonlight on the floor, spilling us in a cocoon of silvery beams. "You've been a naughty boy," each word a swirl of perfumed smoke.

"What's that supposed to mean?"

She shrugs one shoulder. "Someone came to me, told me all about you. You're dangerous. Said I should stay away."

"Someone, eh?" There's always someone ruining it for everyone. "So why didn't you?"

"Because I need you." The way she breathes it makes my stomach tighten, my cock throb, but she's still weeping moonlight as she unrolls little by little, just enough to be safe. "I need a dangerous man. I want you to take me there."

"Take you...?" I know what she means, but I want to make her say it, because I am not going to walk her to the edge of the world and help her kill herself. I'm all kinds of things, but I'm not that.

"Take me to the inbetween, and bring me back, all new and rerolled."

"No."

Oh johnny oh johnny how you can lie.

We walk out together in a night filled without stars. There is only rain and the endless ring of storms that send lightning shivers through the city's skin and neural network, powering the dreams that grew around the grit of some feeb's half-remembered life. Valentina holds my human hand in hers, and this time her fist is hard, sweaty, the moon-coolness washed away by an electrical surge of renewed energy. She's going to die, and she's excited.

"Do you hope this time you'll come back being able to see?" I can't help the curiosity. What is it that makes Valentina hollow?

She laughs at me. "I'm not you, Johnny boy, I'm not afraid of the dark."

I want to argue with her, but I can't. The truth is a glass splinter, too small and brittle for me to extract safely. I have to let it linger and infect me. Instead. "Then what are you afraid of?"

She weeps silver words onto the dark road, and they spell out what she cannot say out loud. We are all, at the end, scared of the same damn things. It's not the dark, or death, or not being who we thought we might once have been. It's the knowledge that it doesn't matter how many people pull themselves together out of the inbetween, how many of us are reinvented, how big our cities get, how real our memories might be, there will always be the Fay. The shadows on the wall, watching us. Waiting. Consuming.

The hollowness inside Valentina is fear. We slip our skins just to keep running from the monsters in the dark.

The inbetween is close now. Just another corner or two and we will turn to face its endless roiling nothingness, the teeth of the storm. The ground beneath feels grainy, indistinct, and the bee-buzz of the end of the world sounds around us, humming into our bones.

Valentina's grip is fiercer, dragging me onwards. I wonder who is escorting who into death. "I'm just taking you to the edge," I remind her. She's already deposited the full amount into my cred-balance. As soon as she's disappeared into the storm, I can turn tail and find myself a traveller stupid enough to take me through the inbetween and into the next city point. Start erasing all traces of this identity and find a new one. "And I'll wait for you."

"Will you?" she asks, one eyebrow raised.

"That's what you paid me for." Take her feeb new rolled-together self back to her home, keep her safe while she's all vulnerable and soft. A little moulted crab. I'm a gunman. No traveller or scavenger out on the edges of New Hope looking for easy pickings is going to approach me. And sure, I'm a murderer, but I gave Valentina my word.

"And what if I don't come out?"

I grimace. "You will."

"So sure," she whispers, mockingly, and for a moment she is Valentina at the bar, smoky smooth, shedding moonlight wherever she goes, and not a woman weeping for things she does not remember.

We have chosen a spot near the foot of one of the vast power pylons that ring New Hope. This one is marked in red painted scrawl, words seventeen foot high screaming out a message to some lost family, lost world.

I WANT IT ALL

A sentiment anyone who pulled themselves out on this indistinct strand could understand. I want it all back, I want it all how it was before, I want it all to end, I want it all to begin.

When she takes a final breath and walks away from me, the world almost goes silent. I sit with my back against the flaking metal, gun arm ready across my knees. The A of ALL towers over my head, a rocket to the stars that aren't there. Overhead the lightning flickers from cloud belly to cloud belly, and the sharp ozone stink burns inside my nostrils. Far away music drifts in and out of hearing, soft swoops of vowels turning to static and hiss.

Valentina's pale dress disappears into the storm, a ghost into black fog. My stomach clenches, and the gun makes an odd noise as the metal contracts. I bare my bullet teeth to the end of the world while I wait for Valentina to unroll and reroll and emerge newly-skinned, rememoried, and for one brief moment; free of hopelessness.

There's no way to tell time in this new world. It skips and shudders and spins at its own pace, but I count out heartbeats, and I wait. When I reach four thousand, I stand, stiff-muscled and aching, and push myself away from the ALL. One-handed, I wrap my white silk scarf about my mouth and nose, and plunge after her.

❋

I've been between and in before. Tracking people the Fay want dragged back to their palaces and their beautiful claws and teeth. But I had protection, the blessings of our overlords and ladies. Now all I have is my gun arm, the rattle of baby teeth in tin, my mouth full of silver casings. None of these things is going to save me if I start unrolling. I pull my memories closer to me, focusing on the things that make me Baby Teeth Johnny with his radiant grin. I was once this man who knew only that I was safe, that as long as the Fay were the fiddlers and I danced to their tune I would be just fine.

If I start to tear apart, how will the thing that was once me know where to return? I look down. In the darkness of whirling soulstuff there are no foot prints. Only faint depressions mark the volcanic silicate and ash, slowly filling as Valentina's path is erased. Here and there are spatters of moonlight, already almost gone.

I draw the rusted tin from my pocket, flick it open with one hand. The baby teeth are tiny opals emitting a candle light glow. Out here in the inbetween the teeth are not fragmented memories, but bits of an actual flesh and blood human being. They were never my teeth. They probably belonged to some child Muse. The dead gods only know what happened to the damn thing. Is it still alive post-extraction, or did the Fay gently skin it and whisper honey words into its raw flesh after? Did they eat it slowly, molecule by molecule? Or did they let it go free? It is too late to save it, only one thing matters now. The teeth will not unroll and disappear.

Carefully, I shake out tooth after tooth as I follow the last traces of Valentina. Each step I take unravels me a little, grain by grain I lose myself into the swirling ash of other humans, my recollections splitting and drifting away.

Valentina is made of marble bones by the time I find her. All the dead skin whipped from her frame, all the weeping moonlight swirled into the dark. I sit with her as she constructs herself anew from memories she pretends are her own. As she grows I disappear. I tell myself I'm stronger than her. I know how to do this. I focus on a memory that I know is mine. My finger, chubby, nail bitten right down below the finger tip, slowly underlining sentences that I sound aloud. The images on the page flicker bright as butterflies, garish, familiar. I hold onto my childhood, my mother singing as she moves behind me. Good things this time, I tell myself. Not fear or pain or loss. I have lived that life already.

Oh johnny oh johnny how you can love.

Bitter confusion fills my mouth, and my bullet teeth fall out, dissolving into the ground. They will be left behind and forgotten. I spit to clear the taste.

"Hey, Johnny-boy," Valentina says. Her hand is naked against mine. "It's time to return."

My gun arm shatters, the pieces flying away on the endless storm, and the past winds itself around my bones.

"The teeth," I tell her. "Follow them back."

The Muse's teeth light our way through the infinite between, tiny shifting comets in a space that no longer exists. As we walk I shed myself, and grow.

✳

It doesn't matter how this begins.

I've had a few glasses of the best gin that cred can buy in Eight to the Bar. I'm not drunk. I'm blinded by my companion. Valentina the sun. She fills my glass from the gin bottle we bought, our conversation threading between the songs the Satellite Sisters – all six of them – are belting out from the tiny stage.

It doesn't matter how many times you've died and died and died again, and rolled and rolled and rerolled yourself together.

Twice, and twice, if you're asking.

It doesn't matter how many times you come back from the dead, you never stop learning.

Valentina's eyes are burning holes, and the light that sears out of her shows every scar and twisted bit of dirt, every torn corner, every line and wrinkle of every face in the bar. She runs her bright fingers down my arm, her nails catching on the feathers that push shadow dark through my skin, and I lean into the touch, soaking up the warmth.

In four thousand heartbeats, we will have finished this bottle of gin, and the sun and I will walk out into the dark and moonless night, and we will fly away.

Cat Hellisen writes weird, lush speculative fiction. They are the author of novels, short stories and poems, and a winner of Short Story Day Africa.
Originally from South Africa, they now live in Scotland where they spend their time walking their dog and figure skating. Cat Hellisen is represented by Portobello Literary. You can find out more about Cat's work at www.cathellisen.com

The Cuddle Stop

Laura Watts

Arrivals was a nightmare, queuing for decontamination. But there was such a warmth to the wooden panels lining the walls. I had to lean in to smell them: printed. In between that thought and the long inhale, I imagined the 'ponics needed to grow pine, bamboo, thick enough to create a veneer. I remembered real wood, bark, the rough scraping of birch under my palm, warm slippery silver, split sharp, opening to the tree core. This station hive has a little more care in its design than my last stop. The label is on the literal box,

Nordbikube, hive made by the North folk. Ship logs it as Waypoint 902. I'm docked planetside, so I get a view of the rock mass to which we're tethered. An errant planetoid with a great gouge, as though its single eye has been plucked out. The rock has claw marks down its grey cheek. Wounded. Aren't we all. Here I will dawdle. Expand and unfurl my limbs, release my lungs, weep until I am dry. Load up and then be on my way, out there, into the star dark, alone again. Ninety-eight days since my last stop, since I breathed the same molecules of oxygen and nitrogen as another human. The next sailing will be twice that length. But not yet. This hive, I hope it goes well. I hope I don't screw up this visit. Space is too small. There are too few of us out here. Folk remember. The older ship mates have reached that irritating level of wisdom and self-awareness where they don't seem to care, appear to accept each breath they are given (or not, when their ship fails). Well, that bitterness is something to note in my next sit. Even docked, I still sit the daily practice: meditate, journal, focus, physical practice, breathe. Breathe. Cool air pressing the cartilage in my nose, a ball of lightness in my throat, filling my diaphragm, pushing my chest out against my suit. Why did I choose this life? To be alone? To be with myself? Distraction: only my second time wearing fins today. The air jets down the channels and combs are ringed with light, but it took me a while to get my eye in, to catch them dotted through the wood print walls. The experienced mates already had the knack to flip the fins on their feet at just the moment to flow forward. They looked like stingrays, bodies rippling in the next-to-zero G. I found a quiet channel out at the rim and hung about, flapping my feet. The jets are so weak, it still feels impossible, you get so little momentum. Must be something to do with the shape of the airflow. I'll try again tomorrow. Maybe. Being a beginner is a definite struggle still. Noted. Moving on. This entry has all been prelude and warm up, of course, to the Cuddle Stop. The best one I have experienced so far. There was a water ball with a granite stone for my toes to paddle with. There was a wall of grass, damp with dew that soaked through my pores. I smelled soil. There was a box of golden brown Chanterelle mushrooms, juicy spores planting themselves into my airways. The main rooms were filled with soft pink, red, and golden glows, and dark cocoons on the walls. This time not looking like internal organs but a dawn-lit cabin. I still feel too new, too afraid of the subtle etiquette to join the community and cover others, but I climbed into a cocoon and just waited, smelling basil, jasmine, rose. Someone came over and offered a cuddle. They were middle-aged with kind eyes, an older ship's mate. I took a breath and accepted. I felt their warm body mass press against mine as they pulled forward, their chest connecting to my chest, human to human, there was the almost forgotten shape of a person shadowed in front of me. Our suits and the thick cocoon spreading warmth without contact. Their body tapered to a polite nothing below their waist. They rested their head against mine, dark arms around my shoulders, and through our silken masks I felt their ear against my ear, the folds of their arching helix. The arch of an ear beside mine. I sucked at them with my soul. There was the inevitable sobbing. I unravelled my loneliness, that pain which sits like a neutron star, a burning black hole between my shoulder blades. It's pulling on my spine, now, as I write. A weight pressing on my lungs during the days alone. Then, today, I let it flare out with a cry. Why do I do this to myself? Why do I choose this? Keep making this choice? Why do I sit alone in the void, seeking and failing to find some wisdom? Why do I attempt to look at myself, just for who I miserably am? Allow myself to spend days wallowing, wishing I was less wounded, less broken, just... less. I do this in return for servicing the ship. *Your days are in service to the universe*, they said. I took the oath. I wish I was less ambitious, honourable, curious, whatever it is that keeps me in service. Note that I do not know. I cannot admit it. Not yet. I cuddled another human being today, a stranger, feeling the possibility and absence of skin. Skin: soft and brown, gnarled and yellow, veined and pale. I dream of skin. Arteries pulsing, joules of heat, almost impossible in our microbe-separated lives. Still they, that kind person, touched me, reached out, cuddled me, until they pulled back with a cool release that felt like the kick of a lover's rejection. Lover? Will I ever experience intimacy again? There is little hope for that. Distraction: there is the bass thrum of the ship, around me, holding me in my bunk. Here are the hairs on my arm, raising as I brush them with my fingertips. I run my middle finger over the dip in my clavicle, around my collar bone, down, spread my hand, hover it over my breast, my heart. All my fingers are alive now. My skin tingling, pulling, nerve endings yearning. I blow through my mouth, feel my lips flutter. I lift my other hand and trace my cheek, along my bone, to my ear, follow the angle down to my jaw line, out to my chin and up and over my lower lip, to where my skin turns wet and glistening smooth. This, perhaps, is an answer. This is why I choose to service the ship and sail alone through the starlit dark. Because sometimes, like now, I can feel this sharp, this solid, this attuned, this whole. I can feel. Really feel. Here I am. Here in the dark I will always be.

Laura Watts is an author, poet, and ethnographer of futures, based in Orkney, Scotland. Her latest book, *Energy at the end of the World* (MIT Press), is part popular science, part rural fantasy, and was longlisted for the Highland Book Prize and shortlisted for Saltire Research Book of the Year.

Targets

Eric Brown

I **was watching the three-dee with Kelly** when the programme was interrupted.

"Uh-oh," she said.

I gripped her hand. "Don't worry."

She turned and stared at me, the hologram pulsing on her forehead.

I stared at the three-dee in the corner. The frame was empty; then a tall man in a black suit appeared.

Kelly began to weep.

The suit said, "Citizens, your son, Edward, has been selected by LAPD for immediate targeting. Please make an appointment at your closest LAPD clinic within the next five days. I will now return you to *Sunny Days in Idaho...*"

Kelly jumped up and crossed to the bedroom door. I joined her, staring in at our sleeping son. He was curled up, warm and dreaming. Innocent.

"Was I a fool, Joe, for thinking…?"

I scratched my forehead where the hologram was. "We *both* hoped, Kelly. We dreamed."

I wondered at the chances of the child of two targets being selected. A statistical anomaly, I told myself.

We killed the three-dee and went to bed.

I couldn't sleep. At two, with Kelly sound asleep beside me, I rolled out of bed, dressed quietly and left the apartment.

It was a risk. Venturing out after dark was always a gamble for people like me and Kelly – and for Edward, now. But I needed a drink; more, I needed to talk.

I kept to the shadows, skulking like a rat. I knew where the night cops usually patrolled, but you could never be sure. Sometimes they liked to ring the changes, to keep people like me on their toes.

The bar wasn't signed. It was underground, literally. I crept down the steps, entered the code on the door and slipped inside.

It was like coming home.

A dozen people like Kelly and me, holograms glowing in the semi-darkness, sat quietly drinking.

I ordered a beer and drank. Thirty minutes later, I ordered another. I felt a little better then. At three, Al came in, fresh off his night shift.

"Hey, my friend." He clapped me on the shoulder. "Whatcha doin' here?"

I told him about Ed's selection.

He pulled a face. "Hey, that's tough. I'm sorry. How's Kelly?"

I shrugged. "Cut up. What do you expect?"

"That's life, Joe. We gotta learn ta live with it."

"Yeah," I said, and bought a couple of drinks. "Shit."

A few beers later, I staggered home. I kept to the shadows, but I wasn't afraid now. Dutch courage. Let the cops shoot me. Only tomorrow, when I'd sobered up, would I regret my foolishness, regret potentially making Kelly a widow at twenty-three.

So we took Ed to the LAPD clinic, and a blank-faced nurse zapped our son with the laser and a neat, round hologram target implanted itself in the centre of his forehead.

Our life changed, after that. No more risks. With Ed's welfare to think of, we imposed a curfew on ourselves. Never go out after sunset, only during the day; keep to busy areas. Avoid patrol cars, and don't *ever* go anywhere near police stations.

We got by.

Ed was bullied at school, of course. I remember the time I'd been singled out for the hologram on my forehead, and I felt powerless to help him. Words were useless. He had to learn to look after himself, just as Kelly and I, and all the others had done.

He grew into a great kid.

One day – he was around seven, eight – he came in after school and said, "Dad, I want to be a teacher when I grow up."

I could have wept. "That's great, Ed."

I glanced into the kitchen to see if Kelly had heard. She was facing the sink, her back tensed.

He'll forget the ambition in time, I told myself, move on to something else.

That night, in bed, Kelly said, "You gonna tell him he can't be a teacher?"

Years passed. We survived. I got a little heavier. My job at the landfill was steady. Kelly moved from Walmart to Safeway.

We began to think about what Ed might do when he left school at fifteen. I had a word with my boss, trying to get him a place at the landfill. Kelly's boss said there might be an opening stacking shelves in a few years.

One night, I was late back from the landfill. Just twenty minutes, but it nearly cost me my life. I was turning the corner to my block when I heard an engine behind me. The car was crawling along. My belly flipped.

I didn't turn, just walked faster.

The car drew alongside. A cop car.

Oh, Christ...

The driver said, "Stop right there and turn around real slow."

I did that.

The fat cop grinned. "Hey, look what we got ourselves here, Gene. If it ain't a fuckin' target."

His partner leaned forward, took a long look at me.

The driver said, "ID."

I passed him my card.

He scanned it, passed it back. I could see him calculating. Shoot me now, through the head, or have a little fun, let me run and get me in the back...?

"You work at Macready's landfill?"

"That's right, sir."

He said to his buddy, "We ain't stiffed no one from the 'fill in years, have we?"

"Don't think we have at that," Gene said.

He passed me my ID. "Off you go, boy."

I turned, shaking, and began walking. I thought of Kelly, making dinner at home. I thought of Ed, and the girl he'd been seeing lately...

I tensed myself for the bullet. *Just make it quick,* I thought. *In the head...*

The cop car started up. Caught up with me and drove alongside. The driver laughed. "Your lucky day, boy! You thank your fuckin' god I ain't in the mood."

They drove off, laughing, and it was all I could do to stop myself yelling obscenities after the bastards.

Ed was thirteen when he came home one day and said, "Dad, it's unfair."

I shrugged. "Life is unfair, Ed."

"But *why*...?"

"The country's overpopulated, Ed. The cops need to meet their quota."

"I suppose I meant... why me? Why us?"

I didn't like the whine in his voice. I shrugged again. "Why not? Life's a lottery. You take the good with the bad. It's no good complaining."

"But..."

"There's nothing you can do," I said. "End of. Learn to live with it. Do you hear your mom complain? Me?"

"I just wish..."

I sighed. "Try not to wish, Ed," I said. "Just accept."

Life wasn't that bad. We had the apartment. It was warm in winter, cool in summer. I had the job, my friends down the bar. Every month, I took Ed to a game. I felt safe in the crowd. I had Kelly, a woman who loved me, and a son who was growing into big, kind, bright young man.

I watched the news, but didn't take much notice. There was nothing I could do to make anything better. The way I looked at it, the world had always been going to hell in a handcart – so why worry? Just accept.

Ed left school and got a job at Safeway. He walked in every morning with Kelly, and came back with her at six. The extra income bought us a few luxuries: takeaways at the Thai place that had just opened along the block, and a subscription to one of the big cable channels

I was fifty, and I'd never been happier in my life.

One day, Kelly and Ed were late back from work.

I tried not to worry, but they were *never* late.

I called Kelly's cell phone. No reply. The same with Ed's.

Six-thirty came and went, then seven. I tried calling them again.

I turned on the three-dee, tried to watch a documentary about the Arctic.

Jesus... Eight o'clock.

They'll be fine, I told myself. Kelly's just got herself some overtime, that's all, and Ed's helping her, and they're so damned busy they haven't had time to call.

Then the image of the Arctic faded.

I stared at the guy in the black suit, my heart racing.

He stared back at me. I told myself he was just a virtual construct, not a real person with feelings. But that didn't stop me hating the bastard.

"I regret to inform you..."

I interrupted.

"Who?" I said. "Kelly, or Ed?"

Eric Brown, who published more than 50 novels, children's books and short story collections, died in March 2023, aged 62.

Eric Brown won the British Science Fiction Award twice for his short stories, and his novel Helix Wars was shortlisted for the 2012 Philip K. Dick award.

As John Jerrold, his agent, said:

"He was a wonderful, underrated writer, full of brilliant invention and an innate understanding of characters' flaws and foibles. He will be greatly missed as an author – but even more importantly as a warm, caring human being."*

I got to know Eric after hearing that he lived in Scotland, and invited him to act as a judge in Shoreline of Infinity's first Flash Fiction competition, alongside Pippa Goldschmidt. Eric quickly became a friend and advocate of Shoreline of Infinity, acting as Fiction Consultant to help us seek the gems in the submissions stash.

This special issue gives us an excuse to reprint this story, first published in *Shoreline of Infinity 8*.

We published his serial, *Approaching Human*, online in 2022, and we will be releasing this as a paperback novella in Autumn 2023.

Eric will be sorely missed, and our hearts go out to his wife and daughter.

—*Noel Chidwick*

*The Guardian, 23rd March 2023

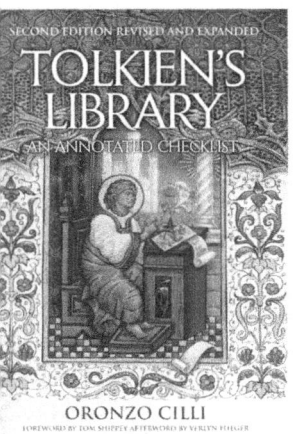

Cymera Festival/
Shoreline of Infinity
Short Story Winner: 2019

A Letter South

Beth Nuttall

Tigh Mor Beinn
Culnaglass
Coigach

12a West Heath Road
Broadmead
Hamps

26th April

Dear Megan,

Thanks so much for the photos you sent with your last letter!
The girls are getting big now – it's easy to forget how quickly
they change at that age, when I only hear them on the phone.
I don't have any photos as we still can't get hold of printer ink,
but I still take lots in the hope I can send you some eventually!

Art: Mark Toner

Spring has finally arrived here, the land has started to turn green and I'm writing this on the slope above the house. Behind me is the immense silence of the hills and in front the silence of the sea, and my hand has already started to go numb because actually, it's still cold.

The wind has dropped so I can hear water everywhere, and birds, and the whumph of the turbine in the distance. Along the road someone is herding their sheep and the boys are 'helping' turn over the veg garden with their usual shouting. But it's all just layers on top of the silence. Even the cars were like that. It would be easy to pretend that nothing has changed, from here. Gives me a dizzy feeling remembering all the times we were up here before.

Yes, it's all very idyllic today although it feels like spring has been a long time coming – maybe I'm getting old... Fortunately the house is pretty new and therefore well-insulated and draught-proof. The older cottages have mostly been abandoned now, or are being used as barns. There were still holiday homes being built here right up to the end, so folk have been able to move into them instead. Some of the more luxurious have hot tubs and so on, though as you can imagine it's quite hard to justify heating that much water :-)

There are still houses that are empty, too.

Sorry to hear about your bin situation – sounds horrible. I hope they've been cleared now, at least it wasn't too hot I guess. Would have been even worse in the middle of your summer heatwave. And I hope Dave has stopped being stressed about the electricity as it sounds like you're managing fine! I can't imagine why he is so desperate to keep his phone and tablet charged anyway since most of the time they're not connected to anything ;-) At least he's flying again now, even if he's getting most of his work from the military. You'd think they'd have the equipment to do their own aerial surveys...

The boys are both fine, in fact doing really well. Luckily for us they were young enough when we came here that they don't remember too much about the things they can no longer have. The teenagers and young adults are the worst – the ones that are left have a constant empty-handed look, as if they should be carrying something important. Actually, they are leaving here the same as they always did, looking for the future they should have had. The difference is that it no longer exists except inside their own heads. Hmm, maybe that's not so different really.

Anyway it's great for kids here: wandering unsupervised over the hills, catching hermit crabs in rockpools, flying kites on the big sand. So far we've managed to get hold of proper winter coats and hiking boots so they've been outside a lot right through the winters. I've lost count of how many old women have proudly informed me that the boys are having a 'proper' childhood, as if they are somehow responsible. And the boys are happy and healthy, and it's all good, but—

You asked if I felt sad about leaving Edinburgh. Not as it was when we left, that's for sure!

Mainly I regret not being able to give the boys the life I expected – all the things they could have done. Theatres, gigs, the madness of the Festival, cafe and restaurants, heated swimming pools with waves and flumes, football matches (though I'm quite relieved that I won't have to take them to any!). They won't even get to go to the cinema. I don't think staying in the city would have changed that. I mean, your cinema and swimming pool shut down, right? Didn't the cinema get bombed?

And coffee. You'd think I'd have got over it after this long.

Finlay's arm has fully healed now, thanks for asking. Luckily it didn't get infected although we do have a doctor here now and a pretty good stockpile of medicines. Seems like someone's still pushing hard to get them manufactured and distributed as they are easily available at the markets in Inverness. I'm so glad you found a supply of inhalers for Rebecca – fairly legitimate this time too, by the sound of it. I was really worried when you told me about being burgled, though I tried to hide it at the time. And the people who robbed you, how desperate must they have been to steal medicine out of a child's bedroom?

Another teacher arrived last month, which is great. She had cycled all the way from Dundee! She's good with the kids, gets on well with Mrs Malcolm. The two of them have some grand plans apparently, but for now they can divide the school between them and focus on a smaller age-range. The problem will come when the first child reaches high school age – at the moment Magnus is the oldest so a few years yet to work out how we can send them to the school in Ullapool. If it's still running by then. If there's any point in educating our children by then.

I've been working on some practical stuff, partly for the school but hopefully for everyone. There was a tiny library in the village hall here, used to be open only a few hours a week. Well, I've been expanding it. It's been very popular! Like you were saying there's barely any tv channels running except the news, so folk here have started reading! A triumph of the power of words etc etc. Or just boredom and a limited number of dvds...

The bookshops in Inverness are running out of stock but there are loads of places to pick up books for free – abandoned charity shops and so on – so I've tagged along on the last couple of trips and now we have enough to fill a whole extra room. Lucky electric cars have that extra space under the bonnet :-)

Everyone else here is either too busy or not interested enough in the endless sorting and running of the library though. It's a bit lonely wading through piles of books on my own. It would be good to have someone to work with.

Stewart and his dad have become totally obsessed with transport over the past few weeks. I know it's really important but if I have to listen to any more dinner-table discussions about how to build a path I think I will go mad! Occasionally they branch out into flights of fantasy about attaching solar panels to aeroplanes or something equally far-fetched, which is even worse...

Actually the path plan, although boring me to tears, is a good one. There's an old postie's path round the cliffs to Ullapool, much shorter than the road. Stewart and I walked it once and it was totally terrifying seeing the gulls wheeling below us while we stumbled and slipped along a 50cm notch in the rock. If we could make it safe for a bike and trailer however, it would mean a lot more people could get off the peninsula a lot more easily.

It would take a stupendous amount of work of course, but there seems to be plenty of volunteers. The folk who lived here before feel trapped without their cars, I think, even though they chose to stay because the isolation makes us safe. We haven't even seen any warships coming up the loch for almost a year. The ferry turned up last week though – who knows where they got hold of diesel! It was full of people leaving the outer islands. Must be hard there after this long. At least we can get hold of stuff from further inland when it's available, but nothing is going across the Minch now.

At the other end of the scale, Stewart and Alex – well, the whole committee really – are desperate to get hold of a plane and a pilot. A small plane could land on the straight, flat part of the road apparently. I can see how being able to fly over the mountains would solve many problems, but I can't imagine how any plane would get off the ground again once it was here with an empty fuel tank.

In the end though, I don't really care what happens to a plane once it gets here, as long as it gets here with you on board. What do you say? I know Dave continues to be loyal to his company but we both know it's only a matter of time before even their little planes are requisitioned. Nobody would come this far after you. How could they get the plane back down south from here?

I've had enough of worrying about you all, enough of being scared that every phone call and letter is the last.

There's space to live here, space and peace. I miss you. I want my nieces to grow up here with us. I want them to grow up.

All my love,
Stella

Beth grew up in northern England, but settled in Scotland a long time ago. She lives in Cramond, Edinburgh, with her husband and two boys. Despite talking about books for 20 years with the Edinburgh SF Book Group, this is the first time she has tried writing a story herself.

Fat Man in the Bardo

Ken MacLeod

A clock ticks. Somewhere, a baby cries. You're in an oddly abstract space, all planes and verticals. It reminds you of a library. You don't remember ever being in a library. You remember nothing but the sudden unprovoked shove in the small of your back, and the precipitate drop. A split-second glimpse of shining railway tracks, wooden sleepers, the ingenious mechanism of points.

Then oblivion.

Now this.

Even here, in this Platonic afterlife, you're fat. You always will be fat. It defines you, eternally. You're the Fat Man. It seems unfair. You don't even remember eating.

Perspiring, thighs chafing in your ill-fitting suit, you set off in search of the crying baby. Your quest takes you around a corner, and at once you *are* in a library. It's no improvement: the maze of shelving seems endless. You take down a book, and find page after page of random letters. The next you open is blank, except for one page with a single flyspeck of comma.

You put the book back in its place and plod on. The crying diminishes. You cock your head, turn, walk to another corner and triangulate. Off you go again, with more confidence.

Around the next corner, at eye level, you meet pair of eyes.

The eyes are connected to a brain, which hangs unsupported in mid-air. The brain is connected to a tiny, tinny-looking audio device where its chin would be if it had a skull.

"Hello," says the brain.

"Hello," you say. You stick out your hand, then withdraw it and wipe your palm on your thigh. Hurriedly, you introduce yourself.

"I'm the Fat Man, from" – it dawns on you – "the Trolley Problem."

"Pleased to meet you," the speaker crackles. "I'm the Brain."

"Yes?"

"A Boltzmann brain," it elaborates. "A conscious human brain formed by random molecular motion in the depths of space."

"That seems improbable."

"*Highly* improbable!" the Brain agrees. "But given enough space, matter and time, inevitable – unfortunately for me." It rotates, looking around. "We seem to be in the Library of Babel, the useless library of all possible books." Its rotation brings its eyes back around to you, and stops. "I keep wishing I could *blink*."

You shrug. "Sorry, I can't help."

The Brain laughs. "Count yourself lucky you're not from the thought experiment about organ donation."

You shudder.

"Well," says the Brain, briskly, "let's see if we can find baby Hitler and calm him down. All this crying is getting on my nerves."

The Brain zooms away, and you hurry after it, your thoughts catching up at the same time. Information comes to you when you need it, yet you have no memory of any life before this. It's like you're...

But you've caught up.

"That baby is *Hitler*?"

"Yes," says the Brain, as if over its shoulder. "Time travellers keep trying to kill him. They always fail, of course, but it's most unsettling for the child. Frankly, I fear for his future mental stability."

From the next aisle comes the sound of footsteps, and a woman's voice:

"Loud and clear, Bob. Loud and clear."

You sidestep between bookcases to intercept the clicking footsteps. The woman halts. She is wearing a dark blue shift-dress and black high-heeled shoes. Over her neat hairdo sits a set of headphones with a mike in front of her mouth. She looks at you with disdain and at the Brain with distaste.

You introduce yourselves. She's Alice. She keeps talking quietly to Bob, warning him against some third-party eavesdropper, Charlie. Otherwise, she's not very communicative.

Soon the three of you find the baby crying in a carved wooden cradle in a canyon of books. You look at it helplessly, then at Alice. She shoots you a baleful glare, picks up the child, and strokes and coos and pats his back. Hitler pukes on her shoulder. Then he stops bawling, but keeps looking around. His crumpled little face glowers with wary suspicion.

Once the baby's hushed, the sound that predominates is the ticking. You listen intently, trying to detect its source. Suddenly the ticking is interrupted by a scream, followed by sobs.

"Jeez!" says Alice. "What now?"

"It's the Ticking Bomb Scenario," says the Brain. "Some poor devil is being tortured to reveal its location."

"We have to stop that!" you cry.

"Why?" asks Alice, coldly. "Do you value some terrorist's comfort over the lives of innocents?"

"*I* was innocent," you point out. "Nobody asked *my* opinion before shoving me to certain death."

You and Alice glare at each other.

"Sounds like you're a Kantian and Alice is a utilitarian," muses the Brain. "The dignity of the individual versus the greatest good of the greatest number."

Stand-off.

"I know!" says the Brain, brightly. "Let's find the Ticking Bomb and turn it off ourselves!"

"Sounds like a plan," says Alice.

The Brain rises high above the shelves, almost out of sight. It roams, rotating, then swoops back.

"Found it!" it says. "Thirty-two minutes to go before it explodes."

"Will we have time?" you ask.

"If we hurry."

Hurry, you do. Alice's heels go click-click-click. Baby Hitler bounces up and down in her reluctant embrace. You're almost out of breath. The Brain darts ahead, a gruesome will-o'-the-wisp guiding you onwards.

You arrive at a wider space amid the shelving, with a table in the middle. In the middle of the table is a box, on which is mounted some kind of apparatus. A man in a white coat is observing the box. Behind the man is another man, observing the man and the box. Behind that man stands ... well, you know how it goes.

From inside the box comes the sound of a cat mewling, a protest louder and more plaintive even than that of Baby Hitler.

"Should we— ?" you ask.

"No," says the Brain. "It would just add another layer of decoherence to the wave function."

"Damn right," says Alice. "No way am I going back for that goddamn cat."

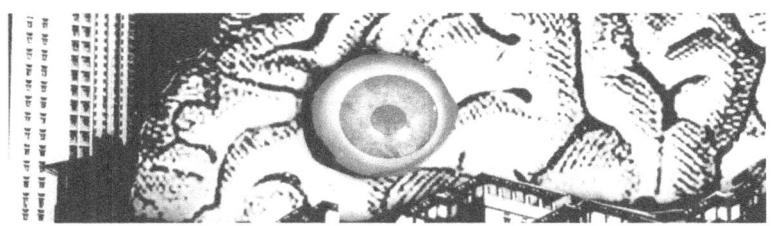

You all hurry on, leaving Schrödinger's Cat, Schrödinger himself, Wigner, Wigner's friend and all the others to their indefinite fate. The Brain leads you around a corner and into an aisle facing a glass wall. The light is ruddy. You spare a glance outside. To the horizon stretch waste dumps, some burning. On them crawl endless human figures, salvaging junk, grubbing subsistence from garbage.

"Is that Hell?" asks Alice, sounding horrified.

"No," the Brain calls back. "It's trillions of people living lives barely worth living! But it's a better situation than mere <u>billions</u> of people living lives well worth living, wouldn't you agree?"

"No," says Alice. "I wouldn't."

"Nor I," you say.

"Too bad!" says the Brain. "The reasoning is rigorous. Your revulsion is mistaken, but understandable. It's not called the Repugnant Conclusion for nothing, you know."

You have no breath to spare for argument. Another ten minutes' jogging brings you all in front of the Ticking Bomb. The simple timer, now counting down from twelve minutes, is attached to a large cylindrical device labelled "10 kilotons".

"Oh!" says the Brain. "It's an atomic bomb! Does that change our views on the morality of torture?"

"No," say you and Alice at the same moment. Baby Hitler's eyes widen and his face brightens, but he says nothing.

Alice reaches over and turns the timer back to one hour. The ticking resumes.

"Now we have time to think," she says.

"It's interesting to reflect," says the Brain, "that somewhere in this library is a book containing a complete system of self-evident moral philosophy that answers all our questions. Formed out of random letters, just as I am formed out of random molecules."

"Along with its refutation?" says Alice.

"Point," says the Brain.

"One of us must stay here," you say, "and keep turning the clock back, while the others go and find the torture chamber before too many more fingernails are extracted. And then—"

"And then what?" asks Alice. "How does that help all the poor people outside?"

"No," you say, "but—"

"Have you noticed how our memories work? Doesn't it strike you as odd? Try drawing something at random."

You find a pen in your pocket, and a blank page in a book.

"What?" you say. "I can't think of anything I'm not thinking about."

"Tree," says Alice. You've never heard the word before. You sketch a tree.

"See?" says Alice. "That's not how human memories work. That's how *computer* memories work, as I'm sure the Brain can confirm."

"Yes," says the Brain. "And?"

"We aren't human minds," says Alice. "We're abstractions of the subjects and victims of thought experiments. This isn't a physical space, and I doubt that it's some kind of afterlife, given that none of us had *lives*. The overwhelming probability is that we're in a simulation."

"Ah," you say. "But—"

"Yes," says Alice. "What monsters the creators of such a simulation must be!"

You and Alice look out of the window at the hellish landscape, and at each other.

"We must put a stop to this," you say.

Alice nods. You reach for the timer at the same moment.

"Wait!" cries the Brain.

Too late.

Zero.

What the Brain was about to tell you is that there are worse possibilities than being in a simulation. The worst possibility is that this thought experiment *is* simply a possibility, but a logical one. From inside a logical possibility, there is no way to distinguish it from actuality. And a logical possibility can't be made or unmade by omnipotence itself, let alone by a ten-kiloton atomic bomb.

What the Brain doesn't know, and couldn't possibly tell you, is that there is a greater possibility: that somewhere, somehow, all the victims of all the logical possibilities including those that exist in what we laughingly call actuality can be saved, can be liberated, can be redeemed; that their suffering can be expunged as though it had never been; and that, however impossible that great, all-encompassing thought experiment may seem, or indeed be, it is nevertheless something for which you are doomed to strive, and to seek over and over again until you find it.

A clock ticks. Somewhere, a baby cries. You're in an oddly abstract space, all planes and verticals. It reminds you of a library.

Ken MacLeod lives in Gourock on the west coast of Scotland. He has degrees in biological sciences, worked in IT, and is now a full-time writer. He is the author of nineteen novels, from *The Star Fraction* (1995) to *Beyond the Reach of Earth* (2023) and many articles and short stories.

The Cactus Farmers

Richard Gregson

The sun rose over the desert, catching the edges of the roof supports in a liquid russet glow and casting a grid of shadows over the cactus beds beneath. The angular geometric patterns made a stark contrast to the twisted, organic shapes thrown by the prickly pears planted in every second bed down the centre tunnel. Between them, the barrel cactuses squatted in their rows; gnarled, spiky, and indifferent.

I took a mouthful of water and hooked the bottle onto my belt before fishing a breakfast bar out of my pocket. I couldn't bring myself to read the ingredients; the 'new and improved' recipe touted on the wrapper was almost guaranteed to be the same appetizing blend of pasteurized cactus pulp, powdered locust, fake fruit flavour, and just enough sweetener to make it palatable. I peeled back the wrapper and took a bite.

Check that. Almost palatable. Oh well.

The sun lifted clear of the horizon as I chewed on the rest of the bar. I shook myself out of my reverie, washed the sticky grittiness out of my mouth with another swig of water and sat down in front of the computer. I tossed the crumpled wrapper into the recycle bin, pulled up the previous night's logs and began paging through them.

To the naked eye, each of Greenhouse One's three tunnels looked much the same as any commercial glasshouse from the last fifty years or so, although their comparatively slender framework would probably have given the game away to an engineer. Like every other modern building, they were riddled with strain gauges, thermocouples, moisture sensors, and everything else that goes into a SmartSuite.

Humidity levels were on the curve, there hadn't been any unexpected temperature fluctuations overnight, and the total collected water figures were squarely average. The pressure sensors told me that the southerly night breeze was beginning to swing around to the west. I tabbed over to the irrigation readouts for the centre tunnel and nodded in satisfaction.

In truth, most of the SmartSuite's capabilities were overkill for a glasshouse, but the water monitoring systems most definitely were not. When every drop of water in the soil had to be accounted for because it was piped in from the local desalination plant, you quickly developed a fine appreciation for your recycling and smart irrigation systems. Forget about spraying water willy-nilly over the beds; each and every barrel or prickly pear in the centre tunnel had its own set of metered micro-dispensers buried next to its roots and hooked up to an electronic management system. Likewise for the dwarf saguaros and the other fruiting cactuses in the right-hand tunnel. The left-hand tunnel ran on a separate closed system – the propagation beds got their own tailored nutrient supply laced with auxins to speed up root development.

I flipped over to the master readouts for the right-hand tunnel and swore out loud. Half of the main schematic was outlined in pulsing red, indicating a blockage or other fault somewhere in the network. A few minutes work isolated the fault to the... *oh great*. It just had to be there, didn't it?

Well, that was my morning gone. I could have waited for Deven, of course, but he wasn't due in till the afternoon shift. According to the manual, I could have left the repairs to him as the senior engineer – the backup systems were there for a reason, and even if they were knocked offline too, the cactuses would survive just fine until we got everything working again. Whether I would survive a day's worth of Deven's patient-but-disappointed looks was another matter.

In Deven's world, you depended on the backups for exactly as long as it took to get the primary systems up and running again, and not a moment longer. I'd never quite dared to ask him whether he learned that the hard way or whether he was just naturally cautious. Either way, he'd been living in this desert since before I was born, so I figured he was probably a good example to follow.

I sighed and hauled out a maintenance cart, dropped my tablet into the pouch on its side, and checked out the tools on the SmartSuite inventory system. I thought for a moment, then palmed open the food locker and retrieved a lunch pack before clipping a rebreather onto my belt. I didn't think Greenhouse One had ever been breached, but there was always a first time and you don't want to be breathing the air outside. Then I began the laborious task of trundling the cart out to the far end of Tunnel Three.

I squinted up at the roof, trying to estimate the time from the sun's position before checking my watch. Another little trick that Deven taught me, although if I ever needed to use it for real then 'running out fast' was likely to be a pretty solid estimate of the time.

The cart wheels squeaked against polished concrete, rumbling over the pipe protectors and cable runs that crisscrossed Tunnel Three's floor. Pushing a cart in here was harder than it looked; whichever way you went, the floor sloped towards a central drain. Great for catching and recycling any spillages; not so great for keeping anything wheeled moving in a straight line. By the time I reached the end of the tunnel, I was breathing heavily, and my arms were definitely beginning to feel the strain. I kicked the wheel locks into place before pulling the workbench out from its slot in the side of the cart and unfolding it. Then I set about isolating the affected cactus beds from the main water supply.

By lunchtime, I'd dug out all the micro-dispensers from beds A through H and had laid them out on the floor on a sheet of polythene. The primary pump sat on the workbench, ready for stripping down. I looked up at the sound of approaching footsteps, wiped the sweat out of my eyes, and waved at Deven. Before handing him my tablet, I cleaned my hands with a squirt of sanitizer gel and dried them on my already mud-streaked towel.

"I already saw the SmartSuite readouts, but thank you. A filter blockage?" It wasn't quite a question.

"Uh-huh. Solid enough that the backflush cycle tripped a fault last night." I watched him page through the system faults on my tablet.

"And you intend to clean the pump and dispensers as a precaution?" Another not-quite question.

"Yup. I don't think there's anything wrong with them but…"

"You want to double check. Very good." Deven's lips twitched in amusement at my carefully neutral expression. "I may yet make an engineer of you, but for now, I believe it is lunchtime. Thorough work requires a…"

"Full stomach," I finished, my own stomach suddenly growling in agreement. "I hear you, boss." I put my tools back in their caddy, fished out my lunch pack, and sat down on the edge of one of the cactus beds. Deven arranged himself cross-legged on the floor, his movements stiffer than I remembered. I studied him for a moment, noting the age spots on the back of his hands and the deep-set wrinkles around his eyes. His short-cropped salt-and-pepper hair seemed greyer than I remembered, standing out against his leathery, dark brown skin.

Turning away before he noticed me staring, I tore open my lunch pack and regarded the oval loaf of pumpernickel-dark bread without enthusiasm. I broke off its top and inspected the lumpy, brownish-yellow contents, my nose wrinkling at the smell.

Spooning up a mouthful of the slop with the loaf end, I waited for the inevitable chilli burn and was pleasantly surprised when my tongue failed to ignite. I read the list of ingredients on the wrapper, swallowing my mouthful before looking up. "They're spoiling us this week. Soya, mushroom, and actual dehydrated potato."

Deven raised his eyebrows. "A new and improved recipe?"

"Aren't they always? This one is almost edible though."

"A pleasant change." Deven broke open his own ration pack and snapped the top off his own loaf. "Yes, indeed. Almost edible. No more than thirty percent crushed insect, I would say."

We finished our lunch in companionable silence. Deven brushed the last few crumbs off his beard, climbed to his feet, and eyed the assorted components laid out on the floor. "How much progress have you made with the cleaning?"

I stood up and tossed my lunch wrapper in the recycler. "I hadn't yet. The stripping down took me all morning."

"In that case, if you don't mind, I will dismantle and clean the pump and filters, while you attend to the micro-dispenser tubing. I'll find it easier to work on my feet."

"Sure." I busied myself unclipping the air duster from the side of the cart, unwilling to meet his eyes. I plugged it in and began cleaning out the dispensers while Deven picked up a screwdriver and turned his attention to the pump casing.

The work was a frustrating combination of repetitive enough to be tedious but fiddly enough not to be relaxing. Dismantle dispenser, test sensors and valve, blow out tubing and nozzle head with air duster, hook up to water supply on cart, run flow test. Repeat with the next dispenser. I was most of the way through the pile when a peculiarly fetid smell rolled over me, almost making me gag. "Whew – you found the blockage then?"

Deven grunted. "And I'll dispose of it through the macerator. I don't believe this will benefit our grow beds."

"Not if that smell is anything to go by. Man, but that's a ripe one." I heard the distinctive rustle of a compost bag, and the stench relented slightly. "No wonder the backflush wigged out."

"Indeed. Have you found any blockages in the dispensers?"

"Nothing that the air duster couldn't dislodge."

"Good." Deven walked over and inspected the pile of cleaned components. "I'll have finished the last filter unit by the time you're finished." He glanced at the sky. "We should have enough time left to rebuild the system before the end of the shift."

He was right – having two pairs of hands to re-plant the dispenser grids made everything else go a lot faster. The outside lights were just starting to come on as we ran the final diagnostics on the newly reinstalled pump. Deven nodded in satisfaction as, one by one, the red warning lights on my tablet blinked out. I watched him unlock the tool cart's wheels and heave it around, trying to hide my concern at the trembling in his arms. I should have known better.

"It was difficult to maintain my exercise regime from a hospital bed."

I stepped forward, one hand reaching out to help, only to pull up short at the expression on Deven's face. The irregular squeaking of rubber on concrete broke the silence and I fell in beside him as he began pushing the cart back to its storage rack. I studied my tablet for a moment, unable to meet my mentor's eyes. "So how was…"

"The hospital? They looked after me well and they don't think I'll need to go back again."

I blew out my cheeks in relief. "That's fantastic news!" A sudden chill ran down my spine. "Isn't it? You don't need to go back because the treatment worked, right?"

"My final scan was clear. The last T-cell infusion was a success, it seems."

I grinned foolishly. "Score one for modern biotech!"

"Modern engineering," Deven corrected me with a faint smile. "Genetic engineering is still engineering."

I was too happy to argue. "A few weeks at the gym to get over the bed rest, and you can think about booking your ticket home!" I paused. "Maybe more than a few weeks. Recovering from cancer and all that."

"Indeed." Deven fell silent for a moment. "I asked about the journey home before I left the hospital. The doctors did not recommend it." His voice took on the clipped tones that I associated with technical briefings. "The radiation risk is high given my age, and my oncology and immunology profiles are both lower-quartile. Hence there is a non-trivial likelihood that I will develop another cancer type. If I do so, then I am a less than optimal candidate for further T-cell treatments and will probably be reliant on medium specificity chemotherapy."

Oh. I bit my lip, feeling the happiness draining out of me. "That's rough, boss. Really rough, I mean."

"Yes, I thought so too to begin with." Deven stared up at the darkening, butterscotch-coloured sky, which was just beginning to fade into the blue of sunset. "But I've been thinking about it a lot. After all, it is not so long ago that people would have been envious of me spending the rest of my days here." He pointed. "And even now, there are not so many people who have seen that."

I looked up, my gaze following the direction of his finger. A line of three evening stars reached towards the horizon, two white and one azure. Phobos and Deimos – fear and terror – pointing the way to Earth. An all-too-apt metaphor, I thought, for my friend's abandoned journey. I lowered my eyes and stared out across the Martian desert, lit by a last sliver of daylight. "No. There are worse places to spend the rest of your life."

Richard Gregson lives in Bathgate, Scotland and works for a Scottish biotech company as an intellectual property manager. A previous job at a crop research facility provided inspiration for the setting of 'The Cactus Farmers'.

The Microwave Library

David Tam McDonald

The Microwave Library sat, on dry days, under a gazebo at the side of number five on our street, which was Roughcastle Court, a suburban cul-de-sac of only seven houses. From the dormer window of my attic room I could see the whole Court, and down the side of number five, the Henderson's house, where the library would sit. The gazebo, legs weighed down by sandbags, covered three bookshelves on casters, each piled perilously high with books. The books were laid horizontally along the shelves, one on top of the other, filling every inch of shelf space, until it was unclear whether the shelves held the books or the books held up the shelves. An old barbecue, with two wheels for portability, sat at one end of the shelves and on top of that, sat a microwave. An extension cord flowed away from it and through an open window.

I had watched the Microwave Library from my window many times though I'd rarely seen anyone use it, and certainly not anyone I knew. My parents, predictably, were scathing of it. Books – real books – were unsanitary, they said, especially when passed from person to person, and since all these books were undoubtedly downloadable these days, the library was only a thrawn fetish of the Hendersons, who were probably virus deniers too.

My dad said he wasn't sure that it wasn't actually illegal, and all it would take would be for someone to borrow a book and then come down with the virus and the Hendersons would be in all kinds of trouble. My mother simply tutted at any mention of it, or its wayward owners. The Hendersons were stubborn throwbacks, refusing to believe that the virus had changed everything about the way we live. They liked holding things, and probably people, in their own, ungloved, hands; they liked going places, and it was a miracle they hadn't gone somewhere and bought the virus back to Roughcastle Court. When my mother talked about them, she looked ill, that pale and sweaty way you get before you puke.

I understood all this, and even agreed, but I also wanted to go to the Microwave Library to borrow a book. Perhaps it was the weirdness of the Hendersons, and their way of living and, no doubt, the idea that I might freak my parents out a bit; but also, I wanted to hold a book. I had never held a book before. Not an adult book anyway, though I had read, loved, and been changed by plenty. I had probably owned some children's pop up books before the virus came, but I couldn't remember, and they would have been disposed of long ago. Somehow, I knew that books were supposed to have distinctive smell, and I wanted to try that out. As winter turned to spring, I watched the weather forecast for a dry spell which would see the Microwave Library come out of its hibernation, so I could make my first visit.

February that year ended with a glorious sunny dry spell which lead Mother to wonder aloud if the virus wouldn't be so bad this year. An early spring might mean an early, and longer summer lull and this offered all sorts of promise, from the long-awaited defeat of the virus to the slightly more realistic prospect of a summer holiday. I'd only had a summer holiday once before and it was another pre-virus experience, I had no memories of. Mother had a sister, my Auntie Karen, in Anstruther – who I'd only ever seen on screen – and in her rare hopeful moments she allowed herself to imagine visiting her. Dad had grander plans: Skye, Loch Ness, perhaps even the English Lakes. The only people seemingly not surprised by the early spring were the Hendersons because the Microwave Library appeared the next Saturday, as if it had been there all winter.

I watched through my attic window as Mr. Henderson dragged the gazebo out onto the driveway. He was in his sixties, rotund and wearing jeans and a Hawaiian shirt in purple and yellow. What shocked me about him was that he had a long, wild, beard. Men these days did not grow beards, as they were a great place for the virus to hide in. It could crawl out your mouth or fall out your nose and snuggle deep in amongst the whiskers, waiting for you to pass it on with a big hairy kiss. Since the virus, beards were beyond the pale, but there was Mr. Henderson with a big bushy one, huffing and puffing, lifting, and tilting and pulling the bookcase over the threshold of his house. Mrs. Henderson appeared to help him: she was ages with her husband, less hefty, wearing jeans and black sneakers. She wore a huge, shapeless, grey jumper on top and had lots and lots of hair. It was all piled up on top of her head with clasps, and undone, it would have come down to her waist.

They went to get the second bookcase, then Mr. Henderson manhandled the barbecue and microwave out and organised the electrical cable, whilst Mrs. Henderson came in and out with armfuls of books, piling them on top of the shelves, squeezing them in wherever. When her hands were empty, she slapped them together up and down the way folk do when a job is well done. Mr. Henderson, took a moment to look at the display of books, kissed his wife on the lips, slipped his arm around her waist, and they both went back inside and shut the door.

I had about an hour before my dad would get up to make coffee and shuffle to his desk. My mother's hours were less predictable. She was prone to attacks of anxiety and sleeplessness which meant she went to bed and got up at different times, depending on how tired and anxious she was. Often, periods of sleeplessness would be followed by enthusiastic use of the treadmill in the living room to tire herself out.

There'd been at least one period of hardcore lockdown every year since I started school; lockdowns where people didn't leave the house for months and when Mum wasn't worrying about the virus she was worrying that we weren't exercising enough and she'd make Dad and I do miles on the treadmill. I hadn't heard her on the treadmill last night, so it was hard to know how long I had before she got up, but this was as good an opportunity as I was ever going to get.

I slipped out of bed, pulled on tracky bottoms, a hoodie, and sneakers. The stairs up to my attic were spiral and open and if you leant on the bannister on your belly you could spin silently to the bottom – which I did. The stairs to the ground floor were trickier. A good few of them creaked and groaned: Dad often complained that I clumped and stomped on them noisily. I crept onto them, pressing my feet to the sides where the wood wasn't so used. The rising sun shone through the glass of the front door making a rainbow which I stopped to admire until the sound of my dad sighing as he rolled over in bed brought me back to myself. I turned the snib on the front door dead slow so only the tiniest click could be heard and crept out onto a deserted Roughcastle Court.

The faint buzz of delivery drones could be heard, hovering above the treeline, waiting for eight o'clock, when they could descend to street level and begin their deliveries. Eddie at number three had a full cooked breakfast delivered every morning, so one of them would be his, full of hot bacon and beans. A jumbo drone had a sack of cat litter swinging gently beneath it, bound for Mrs. McGarrity at number six. I crept along the pavement to the bottom of the Hendersons' drive and then paused, allowing myself a moment in which I might still change my mind. I was interrupted by a knock on a window and Mrs McGarrity was waving to me from her living room. She must sleep by that window – I have never walked past Mrs McGarrity's and not had her wave cheerily to me. I wave back and smile, as that is what she wants, but now, since I've been seen, I might as well see this through. I plough onwards, up the driveway, to the shelves of books

These books are different from the ones I read as a child. They are small and thick and the writing on the spine is tiny: I can't read any of them from where I am standing, so I have to move closer, finally reaching the top of the driveway where I can hide under the gazebo, amongst the shelves and out of sight. I approach a waist high set of shelves, precariously piled with paperback books. I want to touch them and read them but before I can Mrs. Henderson appears, standing the requisite two metres way.

"Hello there, it's Olivia, isn't it?" She is smiling and she is carrying another handful of books. "Have you come to borrow a book?"

She points to the shelves then rebalances the pile in her arms. I just smile and nod, aware that I haven't been this close to anyone other than my Mum and Dad for months, not since the last, failed attempt to restart schooling. Mrs Henderson lollops over and starts arranging the books on the shelves. I pick up *A Clockwork Orange* even though I have already read it.

"That's a classic," Mrs H. says soothingly, "fire it in the microwave if you're worried about the germs."

"Will that kill the virus?" I ask, amazed.

"Who knows?" she muses. "Can't hurt though."

She slips back inside, and the door is shut, though not fully. I lift my book to my nose, to sample the famous smell, but catch myself before inhaling. I take my book over to the microwave. A sign stuck to the top advises just fifteen seconds on max power and to do one book at a time. I pop *A Clockwork Orange* in, turn the dial up to fifteen and press the chunky start button.

A spring tings, there is a hum, and *A Clockwork* Orange turns slowly under a yellow light.

The *DING!* when the timer finishes, is both comical and shocking in the quiet street. I am sure someone will have heard, and they will know I've been hanging out with the weird, dangerous Hendersons, getting myself all germy on books already handled by hordes of people. I retrieve the book and it feels the same as it did when I put it in, I think I was expecting it to be hot or vibrating or something. The cover is glossy but feels furry at the edges where it has worn. There are ridges down the spine and I open it along these and lift it to my face and take a deep breath. There is definitely a smell. I don't know immediately if it is a good one, because it is so strange to me. I guess it is the smell of paper, wood even. I wonder how many hands have turned these pages and if the smell has a little of every person who has read this book, every home it has been in. Nothing in my house smells at all, everything is so frequently sanitised. I am glad now to have the book just for its smell. I close it and put it in the huge pocket of my hoody. Mrs Henderson is looking through a window at me and just smiling. I think she knows about the smell. I wave and take my book home to smell later.

David Tam McDonald is originally from Belfast but has lived in Scotland for some decades now, where he is raising two Scottish girls. In real life he works in museum education. In 2022 he failed to get elected to his local council and as a result should really have more time in which to do some writing.

World of Moose

EDITH

ZARA

The Chrysalis

Laura Scotland

Edith drifted in and out of sleep. She was curled up on the old leather sofa, enjoying the warm, delicate weight of the baby on her chest. The faint sound of the kitchen radio drifted down the long hallway and the bright winter sunlight streamed in through the bay window, forming pools of golden light on the wooden floorboards. The baby was one week old. If Edith moved too quickly the dull ache between her legs would quicken to a bright flash of pain, but she was comfortable now with her knees slightly raised and her head propped up on a cushion so she could see the rowan trees in the front garden. She kept her arms folded protectively round his tiny body while he slept, relishing the tickling flutter of his heartbeat against her chest and the soft wisp of breath on her neck. Tiny white bumps had formed across the bridge of his nose and his papery skin had taken on an orange tinge. The midwife had assured her that this would disappear in a few weeks time, along with the funny little folds of his upper ears, still crumpled from the way he'd rested in her womb. She lifted a finger to gently stroke his misshapen ear, then closed her eyes in the sunshine. The sun was good for his skin. It was falling directly onto the sofa, swaddling them both in a pocket of peaceful warmth, and through her lashes Edith could see the twinkle of damp rowan leaves fluttering in the front garden. Zara would be home soon, but for now it was just the two of them. She smiled, then closed her eyes and slept.

Edith was wakened abruptly by a sharp bang on the window. It was Zara. She was standing next to the rowan trees, peering in from the front garden. Edith smiled at her sleepily, but Zara's brow was creased into an unhappy scowl. She jabbed her finger at Edith and her head bobbed as if she'd spoken, but the window muffled her voice and her mouth was hidden by the black respirator covering her lower face. Edith shifted her body and winced at the sudden rip of pain. The baby stirred and right away she could tell from his tense movements that he was going to cry. His voice flooded the living room just as Zara opened the front door. Edith rose carefully and began gently bobbing him up and down, singing comforting words into the folds of his crumpled ear. Zara's heels tapped loudly on the floorboards as she walked past the living room and Edith listened as she went to the WC to wash her hands. She sang and rocked the baby as she waited, then turned as Zara appeared at the living room door, statuesque and beautiful in her long, tailored coat and high heels. They regarded one another for a moment and Edith felt painfully self-conscious of her creased pyjama bottoms and unwashed hair. Zara removed her respirator but remained in the doorway at an awkward distance. Edith already knew what she was going to say.
"Were you sleeping?"
It was an accusation rather than a question. Edith continued bobbing the baby, using the movement as an excuse to turn away from Zara's piercing gaze. Her dark blue eyes were startling against her brown skin, like tiny panes of stained glass. Edith and Zara had met in Glasgow Cathedral in 2021. Edith had been restoring one of the remaining Munich windows and Zara

had been viewing the venue with her fiancé. It was before the public mask enforcement laws when you could still see the faces of strangers. The light of the stained glass on Zara's smoothly sculpted face had taken Edith's breath away, and when Zara noticed her staring she'd struck up a conversation on Nasir al-Mulk Mosque in Iran. By that time Edith was already most of the way in love, and before Zara's fiancé had finished drinking tea with the priest they'd already had an impulsive but deeply spiritual fumble in the lower church.

Nine years and two global pandemics later, it was hard to believe they'd ever been so reckless. Zara put her respirator down on the lamp table and waited for Edith to answer. Edith continued humming gently until finally the baby began to settle. She felt a small flush of triumph and then turned to Zara.

"I closed my eyes for a bit, yeah. What's the problem?"

"What's the problem?" Zara repeated. "The *problem* is that the doctor said we shouldn't fall asleep with the baby! He could have slipped off your chest on to the floor and hit his head, or you could have rolled over and suffocated him. Not to mention all the germs you'll be passing to him! Haven't you been listening to the news today? There were three more cases of Iberian Measles reported in Fife this morning! We've talked about this Edith, he should be in his Chrysalis!"

Edith frowned, then glanced at the white pod in the corner of the room. It was egg-shaped, about the size of a Moses basket, made of smooth white plastic. On the top there was a touch screen display next to a small window. Along the side, embossed in flowing script, was the word *Chrysalis*. A lump formed in Edith's throat and she rubbed her nose lightly against the top of the baby's soft head.

"He doesn't like it in there, he just cries."

Zara pressed her lips together. She turned to the pod and selected an option on the display. The seal around the circumference opened with a hiss of trapped air, and the top half slowly opened on a hinge. Inside the pod was stark white and cushioned, with sensor pads and a panel of softly glowing screens. Zara scrutinized the interior, then closed the lid and scrolled through the readings on the display.

"There are no faults. All the diagnostics are clear. And it says that he's only been inside for ten minutes today." Zara's paused to raise an eyebrow at Edith. "He won't get used to it if you keep taking him out every time he cries."

Edith looked around Zara's shoulder at the report on the glowing screen and her chin began to quiver.

"I know, but I can't help thinking he must be lonely in there. No one touching him or talking to him. Isn't contact meant to be good for babies?"

"Of course it is, but so is keeping him healthy! Remember what the doctor at the Chrysalis clinic said? It can take time for baby to get used to the pod environment, and some individuals acclimatize more quickly than others, but all of them... do you hear me Edith? *All of them*, do eventually settle in. Babies are remarkably adaptable!"

Edith fought back her tears and nodded as Zara went on.

"Inside his Chrysalis is the only place we can be sure that he's safe. It controls temperature and O2 levels; it filters toxins and micro-plastics from the air; it feeds him when he's hungry; rocks him when he's tired; and monitors his vitals constantly. If he so much as sneezes it shows up on the daily report. Imagine we'd had this technology seven years ago! If every new-born had had access to a Chrysalis pod when Pnuemo-10 spread from Sub-Saharan Africa the infant mortality rate would have been zero. *Zero*, Edith! Five thousand babies died in Scotland alone!"

"Yeah, I know," Edith said.

"And then there was Equine Flu in 2025; that was a complete shambles! The NHS made the vaccine available too early and the side-effects caused more problems than the actual virus!"

Edith sighed. She had heard all of this at the Chrysalis clinic when they went for their consultation. She'd had her doubts about the pods then too, but everyone had been so confident and reassuring, and there had been so many statistics to back up what they were saying. Zara had absorbed them all like a sponge. Edith's doubts had been pacified, but once home her faith in their comforting words had begun to flake away. She turned to

Zara, reluctantly.

"But what about getting to know us? How we sound and smell? How we feel?"

"How we *feel*?"

Edith shrugged. She was starting to feel a bit foolish. Zara shot her a funny look, then swiped at the controls. "Look, if you're worried about the baby getting to know us there's an option to upload photos and voice clips. You could record yourself singing a lullaby or something like that, and the Chrysalis will play it at naptime. On repeat, if you want, all you need to do it program it in. And all of your photos are available, too. Just choose what you want. Look, here's one of both of us from our trip to Shiraz."

Edith shifted the baby in her arms and looked at the photo on the screen. She and Zara were standing in the mosaic light of the Pink Mosque's famous windows. Their hair and skin were stained a multitude of shining colours. Edith was looking directly at the camera but Zara's face was turned, smiling at Edith. The lump in her throat returned and her voice cracked as she spoke.

"I love that one."

Zara reached out and gently squeezed the baby's foot. "Me too," she said.

Edith knew that Zara wasn't really angry. She was worried; everyone was. She nodded, then turned to the Chrysalis and gently placed the baby inside. He made a series of urgent hiccupping noises and flapped his limbs, but he didn't cry.

"See?" Zara said, gently.

"He'll cry as soon as you close it." Edith replied, wearily.

Zara lowered the lid. When the seal engaged Edith felt her insides thicken and turn to something like cement. She could hear his little chirps and gurgles quicken and he began to cry, just as she knew he would, but Zara was unfazed. She adjusted the controls to show his vitals, then lowered the volume so that his voice was no more than a whisper of background noise.

She looked up at Edith and her dark blue eyes glinted.

"Don't look so worried. It's a Chrysalis, not some bog-standard NHS Nest. He's getting the best start that money can buy! Now come on, I'm meeting Sandeep for dinner and you've got that lecture at the GSA tonight. Scottish Urban Landscapes in Glass, right?"

Edith passed her hand over her face. "Oh right. I'd forgotten."

"You'd forgotten? But you've been preparing for months!"

Edith shrugged. She was flicking through photos on the Chrysalis display. She swallowed and then managed a weak smile. "I am ready for it, really. It's a lot to get used to, you know; a new baby. And life just keeps going on as if nothing's changed."

"I know it does, but you're doing a great job."

"You think so?"

"Of course I do! Look, I'm sorry I banged at the window and gave you a row about falling asleep. Work's been a nightmare and all this change is, well... You know."

"Yeah. I know."

"We're really lucky. You know that right? If we were in Eastern Europe or America we would never have been allowed to conceive."

"We are lucky."

"Come on, let go get ready. And don't worry about the baby. I'll drop him off at night nursery on the way to Sandeep's. Don't forget your respirator this time, I don't want another fine!"

"Zara?"

"Yes?"

Edith was still fidgeting with the controls on the Chrysalis, adjusting the colour of the background lighting from soft pink to yellow and back again. She stopped, then stroked the hard plastic of the window where she could see the baby's face, pinched and scarlet from crying. She scrolled through his vitals on the screen, which all read as normal. Finally, she took a deep breath and then turned away.

"Nothing."

Laura Scotland was born and grew up in rural Nova Scotia, on the east coast of Canada. She moved to Edinburgh in 2005 and currently lives in Fife with her husband and two children. Her interests include writing stories, running and travelling.

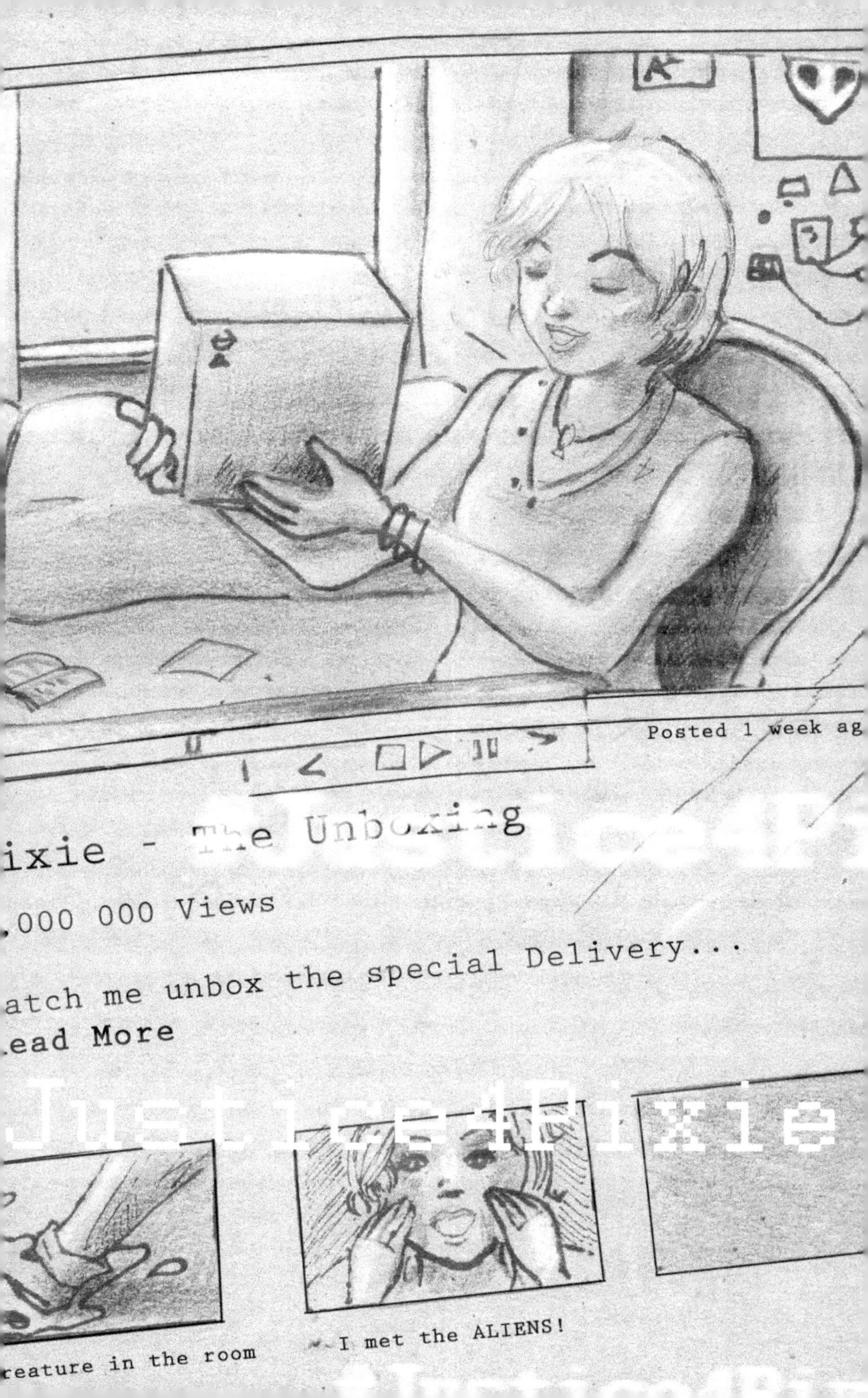

Posted 1 week ag

ixie - The Unboxing

,000 000 Views

atch me unbox the special Delivery...

ead **More**

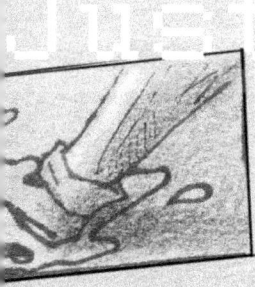

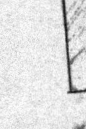

reature in the room

I met the ALIENS!

#NoBadVibes

Katy Lennon

CASE STUDY NO. 89 – LOCAL TERRA YEAR: 2020

[BEGIN AUDIO TRANSCRIPT – ARTICLE TWO]

Hey what's up you guys, it's Pixie! And I'm back with a follow-up video that I never thought I'd make! [LAUGH]

For those of you who haven't seen my original unboxing video, I've linked it in the description box, so please go check it out! So, shit's been going *down*! If you follow me you'll already know all about it, but I just want to address a few things in this video. For those of you who were concerned for my safety, don't worry! I got rid of all the gross, weird stuff they sent me. It's all in the garbage, where it belongs! [LAUGH]

[EDITOR'S NOTE: A full breakdown of the items gifted to the terrestrials in this particular instance is available at personal request. Original transcript file is indefinitely unavailable.]

Art: Becca McCall

You guys had a massive response, my tweet about it even started a trending hashtag, #Justice4Pixie, that was pretty crazy! And listen, I know that everything you guys do comes from a place of love, and shows how much you care about me, and that makes me feel so good because I love you all so much!

But, you know you have to look after yourselves. I heard about a few of you turning up to the alien base, and I know it was just to talk about the box they sent me, but you WILL get vaporized! Too many of you guys have been already, and I just can't condone that! I know you just love me and care about me, but you have to be careful!

And I know a lot of you wanted me to address the death threats? That the aliens claim to be receiving? I highly doubt that any of you guys would do that, so I think there might be a bit of embellishing happening there. I know all of you so well, and I just don't think it's in any of your natures to say something like that.

[EDITOR'S NOTE: In this particular instance, the terrestrial selected for contact maintained a following of over 10 million other beings on her home planet. In this case, individual specie traits such as pride and self-image were not acknowledged. Since then, extensive research is done before establishing contact, making each one adaptive to the life forms in question.]

But maybe they're like, misunderstanding you or something, so I think it's best you don't communicate at all.

Okay, I have a feeling I'll be making another update video about this pretty soon! [LAUGH] so I'm not gonna say that is the end of this! Let's just say they've been in touch, and I think we've found a way to resolve the issue. Don't forget to like, comment and subscribe, thank you guys so so much for watching and I'll see you next time! Bye!

[END AUDIO TRANSCRIPT – ARTICLE TWO]

[BEGIN AUDIO TRANSCRIPT – ARTICLE THREE]

Hey you guys, it's Pixie. So, I'm feeling pretty pissed off that I even have to make this video. It's a complete joke and, like I honestly can't believe we're being treated this way. I've already posted on my daily story about this but it pissed me off so much

I had to sit down and talk to you about it. So, like I mentioned in the update video, I have been in touch with the alien occupiers, but things have not gone as well as I thought they might.

I thought they would apologize for sending me that gross box, and maybe show me some cool alien shit, like let me see into the future or something. They always seem nicer in the movies, even if they mostly ended up blowing us up. I always thought they seemed cool. But they were not like that AT ALL. I turned up to the base and... well there was a lot to deal with. For one thing, they were ugly af! [LAUGH] I thought they might be cute, like little green dudes, but no! Pot-bellied weirdos, all of them! And they were all NAKED! That was pretty distracting, straight off the bat.

THEN! They didn't even want to apologize?! And honestly? I kinda tuned out after they refused to say sorry, that was the whole reason I'd gone all the way over there. They kept going on about using me as a 'beacon' to 'spread their message' to the people of Earth. But I wasn't really listening. Actually, I got to burn them pretty good, I waited until they'd said their whole spiel, then I just looked at them totally deadpan and was like 'So, you're saying this has been a total waste of my time?'

[EDITOR'S NOTE: This response was key in ending the debate in favour of planet liquidation. It is important to consider local colloquialisms when determining a planet's fate. These testimonies can be downloaded on personal request.]

It was so great, I totally owned them! [LAUGH]

They even asked me about that thing in the bottle, do you guys remember that? I told them I found it slithering about my room like a creep and I got my bf to kill it with a shoe. Oh man, they were not happy about that.

[EDITOR'S NOTE: All visiting life forms involved in cautionary missions are now protected under the Life Form as Commodity Law]

Apparently, it was this magic creature that could have cured world hunger or something? Like it shits plants that we can eat? I was like who wants to eat a shit plant though? [LAUGH] That thing was GROSS I wasn't about to keep it in my house!

Anyways, they kept going on and on at me, getting more and more dramatic, saying the 'fate of the planet was in my hands', humanity is 'on a path to destruction', just clickbaity shit like that. They kept asking me to tell everyone to 'change their ways or face obliteration,' I was like, um I don't have that kind of influence, I only just got verified on Twitter. Plus, fuck you – pay me, bitch! [LAUGH] Apparently the whole box thing was their way of connecting with me, to try and get me to spread this message. Um, I think they need new PR staff, tbh! Because that was a hot mess.

[EDITOR'S NOTE: The Visual Warning Law prevented the use of this method, and required all cautionary expeditions to include visual aids as part of their campaigns.]

I just wanted to get out of there ASAP, so when they asked me for my final answer I was like 'Bitch, I already told you! NO!' [LAUGH] After that they FINALLY let me leave. Pretty soon after that, their nasty looking spaceship flew away. I don't even know why, they're so fucking petty.

Everyone in my comments section seems pretty concerned about it, but I don't think we have anything to worry about. We're, like, the best planet in the solar system! Let them go back where they came from, our cultures are obviously just not compatible. For all you haters saying we're about to be annihilated, STFU and get off my page! #NoBadVibes!

Hopefully that should be the last video I make about this whole thing! Thank fuck it's all over with! We can finally get back to the things that really matter. I'll have a new haul for you guys next week! Don't forget to like, comment and subscribe, I love you guys so so much, and I will see you next time! Bye!

[END AUDIO TRANSCRIPT – ARTICLE THREE]

Katy Lennon is a queer horror writer living in Edinburgh. Their work has been published in *Mycelia, Witch Craft Magazine, Malefaction* and 404 Ink's *The F Word*.

The Alien Invasion

Ely Percy

Ah wis abducted by aliens wance. Never tolt anywan but. It wis nearly forty year ago an ah knew whit folk wid say. The wans in ma class wid be aw, Did yi aye? Zat when yi had yir first anal probe? Zat why yir a fuckin space cadet? Probly widda thought ah wis jist makin it up fur attention anyway. Ma ma an da definitely wid. That's whit they tried tae say that time ah smacked ma heid aff the livin room waw after ma da shoved me oot the road ae the telly – they tried tae say thir wis nothin up wi me, that ah wis jist pure at it, pure tryin tae get extra time aff school.

Fair play, ah did huv previous – ah'd a bit ae bother aff Mister Bueller the Maths teacher cause ah twice got caught doggin his tutorials. Yi'd still hink sumdy widda took me tae the hospital though. Ah tolt them umpteen times ah wis feelin weird, an ah'd a massive big bruise on the side ae ma noggin. But naw. Ma ma wis like, Och yi'll be fine wance yi huv an early night. Ma da wis jist pit oot cause he knew he'd huv tae forego watchin the rest ae his Channel Four darts tournament. Aye that wull be right, he roart, Ah'm no traipsin aw the way tae the Southern General fur you ya meladramatic wee shite.

No that ma da ever did anythin tae strain hissel. He'd never worked since he left the John Neilson, an his greatest claim as a faither wis the story ae how he used tae take us tae this Buck Rogers restaurant in Glasgow when ah wis a wean. Yi wantet tae see the inside ae this gaff, he'd say whenever he'd an audience, It wis aw done up lik a space-ship – pure brilliant so it wis – an the fid wis served by actual robots an the real waitresses wur dressed as aliens! Accordin tae ma da, ah pure loved it an ah gret the face aff him tae go anytime we wur up the toon. Ah don't remember any ae this by the way; whit ah dae remember is gettin took tae some clatty burger place where the flairs wur aw sticky an thir wis hardly any light; ah got papped in front ae a big projector screen that played reruns ae the same shitey TV show, week in week oot, whilst he got pished wi his pals at the bar.

When ma parents finally phoned an ambulance fur us, it wis a full two days later, an only because ah took a mad seizure whilst helpin ma ma prepare the totties fur wur Sunday dinner. It wis horrible tae see, she said, Yi wur on the flair jerkin away good style still haudin ontae the peeler an yi endet up gougin a big skliff a skin aff yir ain chin. Aye horrible, mumbult ma da, who'd missed the full drama because he'd been watchin V: The Final Battle.

Ma da used tae be heavy intae aw the auld sci-fi programmes – Star Trek, Mork An Mindy, Dr Who, you-name-it; V wis his favourite though, an he'd aw the episodes on Betamax; he also had a signed photie ae Jane Badler aka Diana the evil Visitor that wis his pure pride an joy. After ah hud ma heid injury he startet askin me tae sit an watch his programmes wi him. Ah wisnae really interestet especially since ah'd a constant heidache an ah couldnae concentrate on anythin fur mair than a few seconds, but ah didnae want tae upset him so ah jist did it. Ah knew he felt bad aboot whit he'd done tae me – the doctors said ah'd a fracturt skull an it'd take six months tae heal, but luckily they didnae hink ah'd need invasive surgery; they also said ah'd probly always be left wi slight brain damage. Ma da didnae actually apologise as such, but he chucked the bevvy awthegether, an never wance did he lift his haun tae me again.

Yir probly wonderin by noo whit this has got tae dae wi an alien abduction. Ah like tae hink that everyhin happens fur a reason, an the only reason it happent tae me wis because ah wis doggin school the day the aliens appeart.

Ah'd been sent tae see an educational psychologist yi see. Cannae mind when exactly… a month later… two months… possibly mair… The doctors said ah wis sufferin fae baith post-traumatic an anterograde amnesia as well as other hings. Magine huvin two amnesias? Fuckin nae luck ataw, eh? Anyway, this psychologist come intae the school – she wis wan nosey bastart, pure askin a mullion questions aboot how did ah find ma school work, an how wis ah gettin on wi ma teachers an the other wans in ma class. Noo, ah might no be Brain A Britain but am no *that* stupit – ah knew if ah said anythin aboot the wans in ma class that laughed an slapped thir hauns at me, or the teachin staff who looked the other way, ma life widnae be worth livin. So, ah tolt her everyhin wis fine; ah tolt her ah forgot stuff sometimes, an ah gied her a few examples ae me bein a pure idiot, an she seemed quite happy at that. Then on the mornin ae that second psychology appointment, ah did whit ah always used tae dae whenever ah didnae want tae go tae school – ah kiddet on ah wisnae well – then ah waitet tae ma ma went oot tae her cleanin job, an ma da went doon the bookies, an ah snuck oot tae the Robbie Park.

See tae be honest, ah cannae mind much else aboot that day. Ah wis feelin a wee bit wabbit, an it'd startet tae piss a rain; an wan minute ah wis at the Animals' Corner feedin bits a plain breid tae Sally the goat, an the next thir wis a mad flyin saucer birlin above ma heid.

Yi'd hink sumdy else widda seen a spaceship alightin on the roof ae the hen hoose. Apparently no though. It wisnae whit yi'd caw a subtle entrance either, whit wi aw the squawkin an the shriekin. Tae be fair, it wisnae a very big spaceship – aboot the size ae wur livin room – an it wis a right dreich mornin, an thir wurnae much folk oot an aboot. But still.

Ah'd this sudden blindin heidache right as ah wis lookin up at the thing, followed by another wan ae they stupit fits. When ah woke up ah wis lyin on a gurney an wearin whit looked lik a metal colander roon the tap ae ma heid.

Noo, ah know whit yir probly hinkin. Yir hinkin, Brain injury equals fuckin doolally. Aye, mibby yir right. Mibby ah'm are an extra-special-terrestrial, a weirdo, a queerie lik aw the cunts fae school kept sayin. An mibby ah don't know every single detail ae whit happent tae me that day. But ah'm wan hunner percent positive they wur real aliens ah saw, an that they aliens saved ma life.

Ah felt much better after the aliens unclamped the mad colander fae ma napper an beamed me back doon tae street level. Ah still couldnae concentrate great an ma memory wis the same swiss cheese – but the dizziness, an the nausea, an the constant poundin ah'd hud in the back ae ma skull fur months wis totally gone.

When ma da come oot the bookies he fun me sittin on a waw roon the back ae the Renfra toon hall: ah'd a bottle ae Strike Cola, three big pickles, an a bag a chips fae Dominic's; ah also hud nae clue how ah'd got there or whit'd enabled me tae pay fur a chippy.

No long after that, ah went fur a folly-up the hospital. That wis when aw the palaver ensued between the different doctors, because they couldnae find any trace ae a skull fracture wi thir machines. They did two mair CT scans plus an MRI but still thir wis nada. In the end they decidet that thir hud obviously been a mix-up wi the first x-ray, an that thir wis never any damage tae ma heid ataw.

Ah did hink aboot tellin the doctors that ah'd been abducted by aliens. But ah knew it'd be a big mistake. Ah could jist imagine masel bein wheeched aff tae some random laboratory fur further tests; probly some snide wee orderly wid tell the papers an ma full family wid end up wi the News Ae The World up wur backs.

So ah kept it buttoned an got on wi ma life.

Ma memory never got any better, an school remained shite, but ah learnt tae live wi the deficits, an the educational psychologist – who turnt oot tae be quite nice – continued tae request me every Monday mornin fur the rest ae the year which got me ootae Tutorial Maths. Hings at hame wur much the same: ma ma wis still ma ma, an she still never listent tae a word ah said; an ma da wis still a bit ae a dick, but him an me got on a lot better.

An thir wis wan other good hing that came oot ae aw this – ah realised ah actually quite liked ma da's alien invasion programs.

Ely Percy is an award-winning Scottish writer, best known for their novel Duck Feet. Their first publication was a letter in Big! magazine (1994). Since then, they've released a memoir, *Cracked*, contributed many stories to literary journals, and published two novels, *Vicky Romeo Plus Joolz* (2019) *and Duck Feet* (2021).
elypercy.com

SF CALEDONIA

SF Caledonia is a free online magazine and resource of short stories written by Scottish SF writers. This was launched at Cymera Festival on 3rd June 2023

The aim is to be an online space for Scotland to show off its talented community of science fiction/ speculative fiction/ fantasy writers to the world – and beyond.

SF Caledonia publishes short stories by Scottish writers. In the initial phase we will be publishing stories previously published. Alongside the story we will publish a short biography of the writer, and links for more information about the writer and their publications.

Who is leading SF Caledonia?

That's me. Noel Chidwick, co-founder and Editor Emeritus of Shoreline of Infinity. Crumbs, I need something to do to keep me occupied now.

SF Caledonia Origin Story

From the start, we were keen to ensure that Shoreline of Infinity published Scottish writers. Over the years we were consistently impressed by the quality of the stories we were sent.

We also ran an occasional series in Shoreline called SF Caledonia. In this series, started by Paul Cockburn, we explored Scottish SF writers of the past. Paul started the series off with John Buchan – we reprint his original piece here. The series continued under the editorship of Monica Burns, who uncovered a whole raft of Scottish SF writers – known and lesser known. We also covered contemporary SF writers, including Ken MacLeod and L.R, Lam.

This new incarnation of SF Caledonia will be a live, breathing creature, focussing on current and emerging Scottish SF writers.

We feel it's time that Scottish SF had a place to call home, and be open to visitors from everywhere who are interested in Scottish SF.

And to be clear, we are looking for Scottish writers, no matter where they are based.

In time, we hope to establish an entertaining showcase of Scottish SF writings and a live database of Scottish SF writers, past and present.

If you want to join us on this journey, as a writer, a volunteer, or have questions or suggestions, head to the back page.

—Noel Chidwick
Editor, SF Caledonia

John Buchan: SF Writer?

Paul F Cockburn

Despite numerous accomplishments in his lifetime – as a publisher, historian, politician and statesman – John Buchan (1875 - 1940) is chiefly remembered now as the author of *The Thirty-Nine Steps* (1915). Usefully, in an introductory note to the now-classic espionage-thriller, Buchan explained his goal of delivering a story "where the incidents defy the probabilities and march just inside the borders of the possible". Raymond Chandler once declared that to be the perfect formula for a thriller; arguably, it's also an apt definition for the most successful supernatural stories.

Buchan had always been attracted to old legends and secret places, whether in the Scottish Borders of his early childhood, the wilderness of Southern Africa, or the rolling Oxfordshire countryside in which he later settled. Buchan's lifelong fascination with the mysterious, uncanny and inexplicable is most obviously seen in his many overtly supernatural short stories, but even his novels repeatedly reflect a core belief in the underlying fragility of our civilisation, and of other realities lurking in the chaos beyond.

"You think that a wall as solid as the earth separates civilisation from barbarism. I tell you the division is a thread, a sheet of glass. A touch here, a push there, and you bring back the reign of Saturn." Those words may have been put in the mouth of the principal villain of *The Power-Room* (1916) but the concept they describe echoes across most of Buchan's fiction.

It's a particularly brutish barbarism, for example, which we're shown in *No-Man's Land* (1899), in which an Oxford scholar discovers Ancient Picts living underneath some remote Scottish hills. Yet, keeping within those "borders of the possible", Buchan ensures that their survival isn't down to some fantastical device. His university education (first at Glasgow, then Oxford) may have been in the classics, but he was interested in the latest scientific ideas of his time: and, by implication, that meant writing what the American editor and scholar Everett F Bleiler described as "an early example of Science Fiction".

Which brings us to Space. First published in May 1911, the story may now appear somewhat convoluted in its telling, but when you consider the quality of the prose and its core idea of strange and desolate alien dimensions barely glimpsed through mathematics, then it isn't just among the purest examples of Buchan's writing you can possibly read. It's also, surprisingly perhaps, pure Science Fiction!

Paul can be reached via: /www.paulfcockburnjournalist.com

Space

John Buchan

L eithen told me this story one evening in early September as we sat beside the pony track which gropes its way from Glenvalin up the Correi na Sidhe. I had arrived that afternoon from the south, while he had been taking an off-day from a week's stalking, so we had walked up the glen together after tea to get the news of the forest. A rifle was out on the Correi na Sidhe beat, and a thin spire of smoke had risen from the top of Sgurr Dearg to show that a stag had been killed at the burnhead. The lumpish hill pony with its deer-saddle had gone up the Correi in a gillie's charge while we followed at leisure, picking our way among the loose granite rocks and the patches of wet bogland. The track climbed high on one of the ridges of Sgurr Dearg, till it hung over a caldron of green glen with the Alt-na-Sidhe churning in its linn a thousand feet below. It was a breathless evening, I remember, with a pale-blue sky just clearing from the haze of the day. West-wind weather may make the

Art: Monica Burns

North, even in September, no bad imitation of the Tropics, and I sincerely pitied the man who all these stifling hours had been toiling on the screes of Sgurr Dearg. By-and-by we sat down on a bank of heather, and idly watched the trough swimming at our feet. The clatter of the pony's hoofs grew fainter, the drone of bees had gone, even the midges seemed to have forgotten their calling. No place on earth can be so deathly still as a deer-forest early in the season before the stags have begun roaring, for there are no sheep with their homely noises, and only the rare croak of a raven breaks the silence. The hillside was far from sheer-one could have walked down with a little care-but something in the shape of the hollow and the remote gleam of white water gave it an extraordinary depth and space. There was a shimmer left from the day's heat, which invested bracken and rock and scree with a curious airy unreality. One could almost have believed that the eye had tricked the mind, that all was mirage, that five yards from the path the solid earth fell away into nothingness. I have a bad head, and instinctively I drew farther back into the heather. Leithen's eyes were looking vacantly before him.

"Did you ever know Hollond?" he asked.

Then he laughed shortly. "I don't know why I asked that, but somehow this place reminded me of Hollond. That glimmering hollow looks as if it were the beginning of eternity. It must be eerie to live with the feeling always on one."

Leithen seemed disinclined for further exercise. He lit a pipe and smoked quietly for a little. "Odd that you didn't know Hollond. You must have heard his name. I thought you amused yourself with metaphysics."

Then I remembered. There had been an erratic genius who had written some articles in Mind on that dreary subject, the mathematical conception of infinity. Men had praised them to me, but I confess I never quite understood their argument. "Wasn't he some sort of mathematical professor?" I asked.

"He was, and, in his own way, a tremendous swell. He wrote a book on Number which has translations in every European language. He is dead now, and the Royal Society founded a medal in his honour. But I wasn't thinking of that side of him."

It was the time and place for a story, for the pony would not be back for an hour. So I asked Leithen about the other side of Hollond which was recalled to him by Correi na Sidhe. He seemed a little unwilling to speak...

"I wonder if you will understand it. You ought to, of course, better than me, for you know something of philosophy. But it took me a long time to get the hang of it, and I can't give you any kind of explanation. He was my fag at Eton, and when I began to get on at the Bar I was able to advise him on one or two private matters, so that he rather fancied my legal ability. He came to me with his story because he had to tell someone, and he wouldn't trust a colleague. He said he didn't want a scientist to know, for scientists were either pledged to their own theories and wouldn't understand, or, if they understood, would get ahead of him in his researches. He wanted a lawyer, he said, who was accustomed to weighing evidence. That was good sense, for evidence must always be judged by the same laws, and I suppose in the long-run the most abstruse business comes down to a fairly simple deduction from certain data. Anyhow, that was the way he used to talk, and I listened to him, for I liked the man, and had an enormous respect for his brains. At Eton he sluiced down all the mathematics they could give him, and he was an astonishing swell at Cambridge. He was a simple fellow, too, and talked no more jargon than he could help. I used to climb with him in the Alps now and then, and you would never have guessed that he had any thoughts beyond getting up steep rocks.

"It was at Chamonix, I remember, that I first got a hint of the matter that was filling his mind. We had been taking an off-day, and were sitting in the hotel garden, watching the Aiguilles getting purple in the twilight. Chamonix always makes me choke a little-it is so crushed in by those great snow masses. I said something about it—said I liked the open spaces like the Gornegrat or the Bel Alp better. He asked me why: if it was the difference of the air, or merely the wider horizon? I said it was the sense of not being crowded, of living in an empty world. He repeated the word 'empty' and laughed.

" 'By "empty" you mean,' he said, 'where things don't knock up against you?'

"I told him No. I mean just empty, void, nothing but blank aether.

"You don't knock up against things here, and the air is as good as you want. It can't be the lack of ordinary emptiness you feel.

"I agreed that the word needed explaining. 'I suppose it is mental restlessness,' I said. I like to feel that for a tremendous distance there is nothing round me. Why, I don't know. Some men are built the other way and have a terror of space.'

"He said that that was better. 'It is a personal fancy, and depends on your KNOWING that there is nothing between you and the top of the Dent Blanche. And you know because your eyes tell you there is nothing. Even if you were blind, you might have a sort of sense about adjacent matter. Blind men often have it. But in any case, whether got from instinct or sight, the KNOWLEDGE is what matters.'

"Hollond was embarking on a Socratic dialogue in which I could see little point. I told him so, and he laughed. " 'I am not sure that I am very clear myself. But yes—there IS a point. Supposing you knew-not by sight or by instinct, but by sheer intellectual knowledge, as I know the truth of a mathematical proposition—that what we call empty space was full, crammed. Not with lumps of what we call matter like hills and houses, but with things as real—as real to the mind. Would you still feel crowded?'

" 'No,' I said, 'I don't think so. It is only what we call matter that signifies. It would be just as well not to feel crowded by the other thing, for there would be no escape from it. But what are you getting at? Do you mean atoms or electric currents or what?'

"He said he wasn't thinking about that sort of thing, and began to talk of another subject.

"Next night, when we were pigging it at the Geant cabane, he started again on the same tack. He asked me how I accounted for the fact that animals could find their way back over great tracts of unknown country. I said I supposed it was the homing instinct.

" 'Rubbish, man,' he said. 'That's only another name for the puzzle, not an explanation. There must be some reason for it. They must KNOW something that we cannot understand. Tie a cat in a bag and take it fifty miles by train and it will make its way home. That cat has some clue that we haven't.'

"I was tired and sleepy, and told him that I did not care a rush about the psychology of cats. But he was not to be snubbed, and went on talking.

" 'How if Space is really full of things we cannot see and as yet do not know? How if all animals and some savages have a cell in their brain or a nerve which responds to the invisible world? How if all Space be full of these landmarks, not material in our sense, but quite real? A dog barks at nothing, a wild beast makes an aimless circuit. Why? Perhaps because Space is made up of corridors and alleys, ways to travel and things to shun? For all we know, to a greater intelligence than ours the top of Mont Blanc may be as crowded as Piccadilly Circus.'

"But at that point I fell asleep and left Hollond to repeat his questions to a guide who knew no English and a snoring porter.

"Six months later, one foggy January afternoon, Hollond rang me up at the Temple and proposed to come to see me that night after dinner. I thought he wanted to talk Alpine shop, but he turned up in Duke Street about nine with a kit-bag full of papers. He was an odd fellow to look at—a yellowish face with the skin stretched tight on the cheek-bones, clean-shaven, a sharp chin which he kept poking forward, and deep-set, greyish eyes. He was a hard fellow, too, always in pretty good condition, which was remarkable considering how he slaved for nine months out of the twelve. He had a quiet, slow-spoken manner, but that night I saw that he was considerably excited.

"He said that he had come to me because we were old friends. He proposed to tell me a tremendous secret. 'I must get another mind to work on it or I'll go crazy. I don't want a scientist. I want a plain man.'

"Then he fixed me with a look like a tragic actor's. 'Do you remember that talk we had in August at Chamonix—about Space? I daresay you thought I was playing the fool. So I was in a sense, but I was feeling my way towards something which has been in my mind for ten years. Now I have got it, and you must hear about it. You may take my word that it's a pretty startling discovery.'

"I lit a pipe and told him to go ahead, warning him that I knew about as much science as the dustman.

"I am bound to say that it took me a long time to understand what he meant. He began by saying that everybody thought of Space as an 'empty homogeneous medium.' 'Never mind at present what the ultimate constituents of that medium are. We take it as a finished product, and we think of it as mere extension, something without any quality at all. That is the view of civilised man. You will find all the philosophers taking it for granted. Yes, but every living thing does not take that view. An animal, for instance. It feels a kind of quality in Space. It can find its way over new country, because it perceives certain landmarks, not necessarily material, but perceptible, or if you like intelligible. Take an Australian savage. He has the same power, and, I believe, for the same reason. He is conscious of intelligible landmarks.'

" 'You mean what people call a sense of direction,' I put in.

" 'Yes, but what in Heaven's name is a sense of direction? The phrase explains nothing. However incoherent the mind of the animal or the savage may be, it is there somewhere, working on some data. I've been all through the psychological and anthropological side of the business, and after you eliminate the clues from sight and hearing and smell and half-conscious memory there remains a solid lump of the inexplicable.'

"Hollond's eye had kindled, and he sat doubled up in his chair, dominating me with a finger.

" 'Here, then is a power which man is civilising himself out of. Call it anything you like, but you must admit that it is a power. Don't you see that it is a perception of another kind of reality that we are leaving behind us? ', Well, you know the way nature works. The wheel comes full circle, and what we think we have lost we regain in a higher form. So for a long time I have been wondering whether the civilised mind could not recreate for itself this lost gift, the gift of seeing the quality of Space. I mean that I wondered whether the scientific modern brain could not get to the stage of realising that Space is not an empty homogeneous medium, but full of intricate differences, intelligible and real, though not with our common reality.'

" "I found all this very puzzling and he had to repeat it several times before I got a glimpse of what he was talking about.

" 'I've wondered for a long time he went on 'but now quite suddenly, I have begun to know.' He stopped and asked me abruptly if I knew much about mathematics.

" 'It's a pity,' he said,'but the main point is not technical, though I wish you could appreciate the beauty of some of my proofs. Then he began to tell me about his last six months' work. I should have mentioned that he was a brilliant physicist besides other things. All Hollond's tastes were on the borderlands of sciences, where mathematics fades into metaphysics and physics merges in the abstrusest kind of mathematics. Well, it seems he had been working for years at the ultimate problem of matter, and especially of that rarefied matter we call aether or space. I forget what his view was-atoms or molecules or electric waves. If he ever told me I have forgotten, but I'm not certain that I ever knew. However, the point was that these ultimate constituents were dynamic and mobile, not a mere passive medium but a medium in constant movement and change. He claimed to have discovered—by ordinary inductive experiment—that the constituents of aether possessed certain functions, and moved in certain figures obedient to certain mathematical laws. Space, I gathered, was perpetually 'forming fours' in some fancy way.

"Here he left his physics and became the mathematician. Among his mathematical discoveries had been certain curves or figures or something whose behaviour involved a new dimension. I gathered that this wasn't the ordinary Fourth Dimension that people talk of, but that fourth-dimensional inwardness or involution was part of it. The explanation lay in the pile of manuscripts he left with me, but though I tried honestly I couldn't get the hang of it. My mathematics stopped with desperate finality just as he got into his subject.

"His point was that the constituents of Space moved according to these new mathematical figures of his. They were always changing, but the principles of their change were as fixed as the law of gravitation. Therefore, if you once grasped these principles you knew the contents of the void. What do you make of that?"

I said that it seemed to me a reasonable enough argument, but that it got one very little way forward. "A man," I said, "might know the contents of Space and the laws of their arrangement and yet be unable to see anything more than his fellows. It is a purely academic knowledge. His mind knows it as the result of many deductions, but his senses perceive nothing."

Leithen laughed. "Just what I said to Hollond. He asked the opinion of my legal mind. I said I could not pronounce on his argument but that I could point out that he had established no trait d'union between the intellect which understood and the senses which perceived. It was like a blind man with immense knowledge but no eyes, and therefore no peg to hang his knowledge on and make it useful. He had not explained his savage or his cat. 'Hang it, man,' I said, 'before you can appreciate the existence of your Spacial forms you have to go through elaborate experiments and deductions. You can't be doing that every minute. Therefore you don't get any nearer to the USE of the sense you say that man once possessed, though you can explain it a bit.'"

"What did he say?" I asked.

"The funny thing was that he never seemed to see my difficulty. When I kept bringing him back to it he shied off with a new wild theory of perception. He argued that the mind can live in a world of realities without any sensuous stimulus to connect them with the world of our ordinary life. Of course that wasn't my point. I supposed that this world of Space was real enough to him, but I wanted to know how he got there. He never answered me. He was the typical Cambridge man, you know—dogmatic about uncertainties, but curiously diffident about the obvious. He laboured to get me to understand the notion of his mathematical forms, which I was quite willing to take on trust from him. Some queer things he said, too. He took our feeling about Left and Right as an example of our instinct for the quality of Space. But when I objected that Left and Right varied with each object, and only existed in connection with some definite material thing, he said that that was exactly what he meant. It was an example of the mobility of the Spacial forms. Do you see any sense in that?"

I shook my head. It seemed to me pure craziness.

"And then he tried to show me what he called the 'involution of Space,' by taking two points on a piece of paper. The points were a foot away when the paper was flat, they coincided when it was doubled up. He said that there were no gaps between the figures, for the medium was continuous, and he took as an illustration the loops on a cord. You are to think of a cord always looping and unlooping itself according to certain mathematical laws. Oh, I tell you, I gave up trying to follow him. And he was so desperately in earnest all the time. By his account Space was a sort of mathematical pandemonium."

Leithen stopped to refill his pipe, and I mused upon the ironic fate which had compelled a mathematical genius to make his sole confidant of a philistine lawyer, and induced that lawyer to repeat it confusedly to an ignoramus at twilight on a Scotch hill. As told by Leithen it was a very halting tale.

"But there was one thing I could see very clearly," Leithen went on, "and that was Hollond's own case. This crowded world of Space was perfectly real to him. How he had got to it I do not know. Perhaps his mind, dwelling constantly on the problem, had unsealed some atrophied cell and restored the old instinct. Anyhow, he was living his daily life with a foot in each world.

"He often came to see me, and after the first hectic discussions he didn't talk much. There was no noticeable change in him—a little more abstracted perhaps. He would walk in the street or come into a room with a quick look round him, and sometimes for no earthly reason he would swerve. Did you ever watch a cat crossing a room? It sidles along by the furniture and walks over an open space of carpet as if it were picking its way among obstacles. Well, Hollond behaved like that, but he had always been counted a little odd, and nobody noticed it but me.

"I knew better than to chaff him, and had stopped argument, so there wasn't much to be said. But sometimes he would give me news about his experiences. The whole thing was perfectly clear and scientific and above board, and nothing creepy about it. You know how I hate the washy supernatural stuff they give us nowadays. Hollond was well and fit, with an appetite like a hunter. But as he talked, sometimes—well, you know I haven't much in the way of nerves or imagination—but I used to get a little eerie. Used to feel the solid earth dissolving round me. It was the opposite of vertigo, if you understand me—a sense of airy realities crowding in on you-crowding the mind, that is, not the body.

"I gathered from Hollond that he was always conscious of corridors and halls and alleys in Space, shifting, but shifting according to inexorable laws. I never could get quite clear as to what this consciousness was like. When I asked he used to look puzzled and worried and helpless. I made out from him that one landmark involved a sequence, and once given a bearing from an object you could keep the direction without a mistake. He told me he could easily, if he wanted, go in a dirigible from the top of Mont Blanc to the top of Snowdon in the thickest fog and without a compass, if he were given the proper angle to start from. I confess I didn't follow that myself. Material objects had nothing to do with the Spacial forms, for a table or a bed in our world might be placed across a corridor of Space. The forms played their game independent of our kind of reality. But the worst of it was, that if you kept your mind too much in one world you were apt to forget about the other and Hollond was always barking his shins on stones and chairs and things.

"He told me all this quite simply and frankly. Remember his mind and no other part of him lived in his new world. He said it gave him an odd sense of detachment to sit in a room among people, and to know that nothing there but himself had any relation at all to the infinite strange world of Space that flowed around them. He would listen, he said, to a great man talking, with one eye on the cat on the rug, thinking to himself how much more the cat knew than the man."

"How long was it before he went mad?" I asked.

It was a foolish question, and made Leithen cross. "He never went mad in your sense. My dear fellow, you're very much wrong if you think there was anything pathological about him—then. The man was brilliantly sane. His mind was as keen is a keen sword. I couldn't understand him, but I could judge of his sanity right enough."

I asked if it made him happy or miserable.

"At first I think it made him uncomfortable. He was restless because he knew too much and too little. The unknown pressed in on his mind as bad air weighs on the lungs. Then it lightened and he accepted the new world in the same sober practical way that he took other things. I think that the free exercise of his mind in a pure medium gave him a feeling of extraordinary power and ease. His eyes used to sparkle when he talked. And another odd thing he told me. He was a keen rockclimber, but, curiously enough, he had never a very good head. Dizzy heights always worried him, though he managed to keep hold on himself. But now all that had gone. The sense of the fulness of Space made him as happy—happier I believe—with his legs dangling into eternity, as sitting before his own study fire.

"I remember saying that it was all rather like the mediaeval wizards who made their spells by means of numbers and figures.

"He caught me up at once. 'Not numbers,' he said. "Number has no place in Nature. It is an invention of the human mind to atone for a bad memory. But figures are a different matter. All the mysteries of the world are in them, and the old magicians knew that at least, if they knew no more.'

"He had only one grievance. He complained that it was terribly lonely. 'It is the Desolation,' he would quote, 'spoken of by Daniel the prophet.' He would spend hours travelling those eerie shifting corridors of Space with no hint of another human soul. How could there be? It was a world of pure reason, where human personality had no place. What puzzled me was why he should feel the absence of this. One wouldn't you know, in an intricate problem of geometry or a game of chess. I asked him, but he didn't understand the question. I puzzled over it a good deal, for it seemed to me that if Hollond felt lonely, there must be more in this world of his than we imagined. I began to wonder if there was any truth in fads like psychical research. Also, I was not so sure that he was as normal as I had thought: it looked as if his nerves might be going bad.

"Oddly enough, Hollond was getting on the same track himself. He had discovered, so he said, that in sleep everybody now and then lived in this new world of his. You know how one dreams of triangular railway platforms with trains running simultaneously down all three sides and not colliding. Well, this sort of cantrip was 'common form,' as we say at the Bar, in Hollond's Space, and he was very curious about the why and wherefore of Sleep. He began to haunt psychological laboratories, where they experiment with the charwoman and the odd man, and he used to go up to Cambridge for seances. It was a foreign atmosphere to him, and I don't think he was very happy in it. He found so many charlatans that he used to get angry, and declare he would be better employed at Mother's Meetings!"

From far up the Glen came the sound of the pony's hoofs. The stag had been loaded up and the gillies were returning. Leithen looked at his watch. "We'd better wait and see the beast," he said.

"... Well, nothing happened for more than a year. Then one evening in May he burst into my rooms in high excitement. You understand quite clearly that there was no suspicion of horror or fright or anything unpleasant about this world he had discovered. It was simply a series of interesting and difficult problems. All this time Hollond had been rather extra well and cheery. But when he came in I thought I noticed a different look in his eyes, something puzzled and diffident and apprehensive.

" 'There's a queer performance going on in the other world,' he said. 'It's unbelievable. I never dreamed of such a thing. I—I don't quite know how to put it, and I don't know how to explain it, but—but I am becoming aware that there are other beings—other minds—moving in Space besides mine.'

"I suppose I ought to have realised then that things were beginning to go wrong. But it was very difficult, he was so rational and anxious to make it all clear. I asked him how he knew. 'There could, of course, on his own showing be no CHANGE in that world, for the forms of Space moved and existed under inexorable laws. He said he found his own mind failing him at points. There would come over him a sense of fear—intellectual fear—and weakness, a sense of something else, quite alien to Space, thwarting him. Of course he could only describe his impressions very lamely, for they were purely of the mind, and he had no material peg to hang them on, so that I could realise them. But the gist of it was that he had been gradually becoming conscious of what he called 'Presences' in his world. They had no effect on Space—did not leave footprints in its corridors, for instance—but they affected his mind. There was some mysterious contact established between him and them. I asked him if the affection was unpleasant and he said 'No, not exactly.' But I could see a hint of fear in his eyes.

"Think of it. Try to realise what intellectual fear is. I can't, but it is conceivable. To you and me fear implies pain to ourselves or some other, and such pain is always in the last resort pain of the flesh. Consider it carefully and you will see that it is so. But imagine fear so sublimated and transmuted as to be the tension of pure spirit. I can't realise it, but I think it possible. I don't pretend to understand how Hollond got to know about these Presences. But there was no doubt about the fact. He was positive, and he wasn't in the least mad—not in our sense. In that very month he published his book on Number, and gave a German professor who attacked it a most tremendous public trouncing.

"I know what you are going to say,—that the fancy was a weakening of the mind from within. I admit I should have thought of that but he looked so confoundedly sane and able that it seemed ridiculous. He kept asking me my opinion, as a lawyer, on the facts he offered. It was the oddest case ever put before me, but I did my best for him. I dropped all my own views of sense and nonsense. I told him that, taking all that he had told me as fact, the Prescences might be either ordinary minds traversing Space in sleep; or minds such as his which had independently captured the sense of Space's quality; or, finally, the spirits of just men made perfect, behaving as psychical researchers think they do. It was a ridiculous task to set a prosaic man, and I wasn't quite serious. But Holland was serious enough.

"He admitted that all three explanations were conceivable, but he was very doubtful about the first. The projection of the spirit into Space during sleep, he thought, was a faint and feeble thing, and these were powerful Presences. With the second and the third he was rather impressed. I suppose I should have seen what was happening and tried to stop it; at least, looking back that seems to have been my duty. But it was difficult to think that anything was wrong with Hollond; indeed the odd thing is that all this time the idea of madness never entered my head. I rather backed him up. Somehow the thing took my fancy, though I thought it moonshine at the bottom of my heart. I enlarged on the pioneering before him. 'Think,' I told him, 'what may be waiting for you. You may discover the meaning of Spirit. You may open up a new world, as rich as the old one, but imperishable. You may prove to mankind their immortality and deliver them for ever from the fear of death. Why, man, you are picking at the lock of all the world's mysteries.'

"But Hollond did not cheer up. He seemed strangely languid and dispirited. 'That is all true enough,' he said, 'if you are right, if your alternatives are exhaustive. But suppose they are something else, something .... What that 'something' might be he had apparently no idea, and very soon he went away.

"He said another thing before he left. He asked me if I ever read poetry, and I said, not often. Nor did he: but he had picked up a little book somewhere and found a man who knew about the Presences. I think his name was Traherne, one of the seventeenth-century fellows. He quoted a verse which stuck to my fly-paper memory. It ran something like

'Within the region of the air,
Compassed about with Heavens fair,
Great tracts of lands there may be found,
Where many numerous hosts,
In those far distant coasts,
For other great and glorious ends
Inhabit, my yet unknown friends.'

Hollond was positive he did not mean angels or anything of the sort. I told him that Traherne evidently took a cheerful view of them. He admitted that, but added: 'He had religion, you see. He believed that everything was for the best. I am not a man of faith, and can only take comfort from what I understand. I'm in the dark, I tell you...'

"Next week I was busy with the Chilian Arbitration case, and saw nobody for a couple of months. Then one evening I ran against Hollond on the Embankment, and thought him looking horribly ill. He walked back with me to my rooms, and hardly uttered one word all the way. I gave him a stiff whisky-and-soda, which he gulped down absent-mindedly. There was that strained, hunted look in his eyes that you see in a frightened animal's. He was always lean, but now he had fallen away to skin and bone.

" 'I can't stay long,' he told me, 'for I'm off to the Alps to-morrow and I have a lot to do.' Before then he used to plunge readily into his story, but now he seemed shy about beginning. Indeed I had to ask him a question.

" 'Things are difficult,' he said hesitatingly, and rather distressing. Do you know, Leithen, I think you were wrong about—about what I spoke to you of. You said there must be one of three explanations. I am beginning to think that there is a fourth.

"He stopped for a second or two, then suddenly leaned forward and gripped my knee so fiercely that I cried out. 'That world is the Desolation,' he said in a choking voice, 'and perhaps I am getting near the Abomination of the Desolation that the old prophet spoke of. I tell you, man, I am on the edge of a terror, a terror,' he almost screamed, 'that no mortal can think of and live.'

You can imagine that I was considerably startled. It was lightning out of a clear sky. How the devil could one associate horror with mathematics? I don't see it yet... At any rate, I—You may be sure I cursed my folly for ever pretending to take him seriously. The only way would have been to have laughed him out of it at the start. And yet I couldn't, you know—it was too real and reasonable. Anyhow, I tried a firm tone now, and told him the whole thing was arrant raving bosh. I bade him be a man and pull himself together. I made him dine with me, and took him home, and got him into a better state of mind before he went to bed. Next morning I saw him off at Charing Cross, very haggard still, but better. He promised to write to me pretty often....

The pony, with a great eleven-pointer lurching athwart its back, was abreast of us, and from the autumn mist came the sound of soft Highland voices. Leithen and I got up to go, when we heard that the rifle had made direct for the Lodge by a short cut past the Sanctuary. In the wake of the gillies we descended the Correi road into a glen all swimming with dim purple shadows. The pony minced and boggled; the stag's antlers stood out sharp on the rise against a patch of sky, looking like a skeleton tree. Then we dropped into a covert of birches and emerged on the white glen highway.

Leithen's story had bored and puzzled me at the start, but now it had somehow gripped my fancy. Space a domain of endless corridors and Presences moving in them! The world was not quite the same as an hour ago. It was the hour, as the French say, "between dog and wolf," when the mind is disposed to marvels. I thought of my stalking on the morrow, and was miserably conscious that I would miss my stag. Those airy forms would get in the way. Confound Leithen and his yarns!

"I want to hear the end of your story," I told him, as the lights of the Lodge showed half a mile distant.

"The end was a tragedy," he said slowly. "I don't much care to talk about it. But how was I to know? I couldn't see the nerve going. You see I couldn't believe it was all nonsense. If I could I might have seen. But I still think there was something in it—up to a point. Oh, I agree he went mad in the end. It is the only explanation. Something must have snapped in that fine brain, and he saw the little bit more which we call madness. Thank God, you and I are prosaic fellows...

"I was going out to Chamonix myself a week later. But before I started I got a post-card from Hollond, the only word from him. He had printed my name and address, and on the other side had scribbled six words—'I know at last—God's mercy.—H.G.H' The handwriting was like a sick man of ninety. I knew that things must be pretty bad with my friend.

"I got to Chamonix in time for his funeral. An ordinary climbing accident—you probably read about it in the papers. The Press talked about the toll which the Alps took from intellectuals—the usual rot. There was an inquiry, but the facts were quite simple. The body was only recognised by the clothes. He had fallen several thousand feet.

"It seems that he had climbed for a few days with one of the Kronigs and Dupont, and they had done some hair-raising things on the Aiguilles. Dupont told me that they had found a new route up the Montanvert side of the Charmoz. He said that Hollond climbed like a 'diable fou' and if you know Dupont's standard of madness you will see that the pace must have been pretty hot. 'But monsieur was sick,' he added; 'his eyes were not good. And I and Franz, we were grieved for him and a little afraid. We were glad when he left us.'

"He dismissed the guides two days before his death. The next day he spent in the hotel, getting his affairs straight. He left everything in perfect order, but not a line to a soul, not even to his sister. The following day he set out alone about three in the morning for the Grepon. He took the road up the Nantillons glacier to the Col, and then he must have climbed the Mummery crack by himself. After that he left the ordinary route and tried a new traverse across the Mer de Glace face. Somewhere near the top he fell, and next day a party going to the Dent du Requin found him on the rocks thousands of feet below.

"He had slipped in attempting the most foolhardy course on earth, and there was a lot of talk about the dangers of guideless climbing. But I guessed the truth, and I am sure Dupont knew, though he held his tongue...."

We were now on the gravel of the drive, and I was feeling better. The thought of dinner warmed my heart and drove out the eeriness of the twilight glen. The hour between dog and wolf was passing. After all, there was a gross and jolly earth at hand for wise men who had a mind to comfort.

Leithen, I saw, did not share my mood. He looked glum and puzzled, as if his tale had aroused grim memories. He finished it at the Lodge door.

"... For, of course, he had gone out that day to die. He had seen the something more, the little bit too much, which plucks a man from his moorings. He had gone so far into the land of pure spirit that he must needs go further and shed the fleshly envelope that cumbered him. God send that he found rest! I believe that he chose the steepest cliff in the Alps for a purpose. He wanted to be unrecognisable. He was a brave man and a good citizen. I think he hoped that those who found him might not see the look in his eyes."

'Space' was published in *The Moon Endureth—Tales and Fancies*, published in 1912. This version of the story was taken from Project Gutenberg.

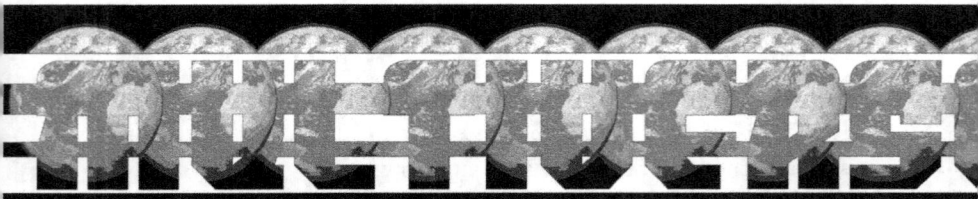

It's with sadness that we say cheerio to Russell Jones, who has been woven through the fabric of Shoreline of Infinity since Issue 1. We wish him well as he moves onto greater and more wond'rous things.

One of his last duties as Poetry Editor was to select three Scottish poets for this SF Caledonia special. We leave Russell with the last words.

A farewell from Russell Jones (Poetry Editor, Deputy Editor, Events Manager of Shoreline of Infinity 2015-2023)

In March 2015 I met up with a strange but enthusiastic fellow in a church café in Edinburgh. The man was Noel Chidwick, and I wanted to give him a few science fiction poems to include in his soon-to-be-published sparkly new SF magazine, Shoreline of Infinity. One thing led to another of course, and within an hour or so, I was the newly-appointed Poetry Editor of the magazine. It wasn't long after that, having also met with the wonderful and equally strange Mark Toner, that I also took on the mantle of Deputy Editor.

In SF-style: flash forward eight years. We've published numerous books and well over 30 magazines, the majority of which included SF poetry. In the magazines alone we have published around 100 poets from all around the blue-green speck that we call home, not to mention dozens of poets in our Multiverse international SF poetry anthology. I also took on the role of Events Manager in that time and have put on approximately 80 live SF-themed events in Scotland and online (every event including at least one poet, and countless bad jokes for which I can now – finally – apologise).

So, if *Shoreline of Infinity* is any measure, science fiction is alive and kicking – both on the page and on the stage. After almost a decade at these helms, I have decided to bid farewell to the good ship Shoreline in search of brave new worlds and words. It's time for someone new to bring their literary preferences, contacts and (dare I say it...) expertise to the next generation of readers and audience-goers.

I want to add a big thank you to all the Shoreline team of course, but also to all our writers, performers, listeners and readers, without whom none of this would have been possible. I'll still be around, skulking in corners and making bad puns. Say hello now and again. Bring me treats. And of course, I'll have a Shoreline of Infinity in hand – I can't wait to see where it ventures next into the great unknown. Hasta la vista, baby.

Pulses

Louise Peterkin

We hoped for surfeit, epic globes, a bounty
so ribbed and basketballed,
uprooting it would launch us backwards,
making soil-angels in the rich pudding earth,
clutching the yield to our chests like kids
we had saved from drowning. We trusted
our harvest would be whimsical; carrots
bearded like Border Terriers, veg so fertile
it frowned like a facial composite. To claim
we got the opposite would not be the full story
but we were gloomy then, ambitions of first prize
fete rosettes crumbling as the spade clanged
out another return of dull chaffs
like dried bugs from a family heirloom. For once
we had enjoyed a common goal, a shared hobby.
Had planned, laboured, feeding
our allotted ground with mounds of kelp,
pounded egg shell, dark tea bogged down to molasses.
We stared mournfully at the disturbed plot,
assessing the drab lot at our feet, the conception
that what we had reaped was not what we'd sowed.

That evening we made supper from our gleanings,
joking about sows ears and silk purses,
but were muted as the huge pan bubbled
under the harsh kitchen light.
I held up the crooked husk;
a weird, long, dishwater thing,
knuckled like a finger; new born; senescent. Afterwards
as we lay in bed, I thought of the beans
rolling round our plates, their alien autopsy colour.
It was then I was jolted by an oscillation inside me,
a throb like a smothered orchestra. You stirred
on your side and I placed my splayed palm
across your belly – a middle aged man's paunch,
stretched from years of home brew.
But the swelling felt different:
tighter, somehow significant. And I felt it in you:
that same strange movement, undulation. I timed
our two throbbings till they rhythmed in tandem
then dropped off to a deep sleep, comforted
by our peas-in-a-podness, dreaming of surfeit.

My Father's Sci-Fi

Louise Peterkin

Hard backed, jam-packed in condiment colours: cocktail sauce, Colman's Mustard. A sepia tang rose from inside, pages the colour of old men's fingers. Time travel of deflated prices: 80p for a novel, more in US/ Canadian dollars. Kneeling at the shelf behind the sofa I fought the tedium of long afternoons slack as space; the drowsy clock; sear of sad, squandered sun on my back. My father lay dozing. Sometimes, his snoring would stop and I counted the s e c o n d s a sick fear he was dead making my toes tingle. Only his Norse blasts resuming released my own breathing, the task of the antiquarian. Philip K. Dick. Dunes sprawling dynasty. Asimov's mysteries – taut and lovely – a box of gems held up with tweezers in a stark white light, the jeweller a squinting cyclops. I liked Bradbury, collections compiled from 50's magazines. The best story hurled me

like a pod from a spaceship into a vacuum of infinite dark folded onto itself like velvet with absolutely no

stars. A man on a long haul space flight. He was convinced his sole companion, Wilbur, was an android, assigned to save his mind from the crumble of solitary confinement. Wilbur was detached, aloof, impersonal. Our narrator: charismatic, inquisitive, jovial.

Then they switched him off. They. Switched. Him. Off. The narrator was the robot all along.

That was a kick in the guts.

That was when I realised there were stairs in my head and I had to stare straight ahead not to tumble down them, get smashed at the bottom.

The covers were frightening: A prickly jewel stared out from one, a sort of pincushion with eyes hanging in a sea of yellow. The worst was a man with a bald head cracked at the top like a boiled egg, out of which rose a moth. The moth rising out of the man's head had a man's head. And it was bald as an egg, cracked at the top with a moth rising out. The moth had the face of a man's bald egg head, cracked...

Louise Peterkin has had poems featured in various publications including *The Dark Horse, New Writing Scotland* and *The North*. In 2016 she won a New Writers Award for poetry from the Scottish Book Trust. She lives and works in Edinburgh.

Captain Kirk visits the Oxgangs Mum and Baby Group

Rachel Plummer

He doesn't have a baby. It's awkward.

He talks into an out-moded flip phone
which he holds in front of his mouth
the way people used to do when we thought
mobile phone signal gave you brain cancer.

A baby gargles. Kirk leans towards the mother.
"I think that's Klingon for
TODAY IS A GOOD DAY TO DIE,"
he says helpfully.

The mother must be a Vulcan. She seems unimpressed.

He can't cross his legs properly in the tight lycra uniform
and he doesn't know any of the words to 'Wind the Bobbin Up'
but he makes the tea without complaint
after that first day when he'd asked why
they didn't just get one of the yeomen to do it
and they made him write an apology letter to Janice Rand.

Sometimes the children cry, and there's nothing he can do to stop it.
Sometimes they won't eat, and the mothers let loose
the words 'failure to thrive' like a bank of phaser fire.
Kirk learns helplessness. He finds himself
waking at night in the red light of his Captain's quarters
as if there's someone crying for him.

He comes red-eyed to the group and his weariness is
mirrored in the women's faces:
worry lines, sagging gut, greying hair, inability
to cope.

They talk a lot about childbirth. More than one woman
is still bleeding. Kirk can't quite keep
the horrified expression from his face
and he's not sure if he wants to call Bones
or his mom, Winona, and tell her
he's sorry for every scar he's ever given her.

He tries to help out with the kids
but he's lightyears out of his depth.

On more than one occasion he contemplates the legality
of using a phaser set to a mild stun
on a toddler who won't sleep.

In the end he's asked to leave when one of the babies' first words is
KHAAAAAAAANNN!

He takes it well. More than anyone,
Kirk knows things are tough on life's frontiers,
where if you're going to go you might as well go boldly,
these places where no man.

Captain Kirk visits Edinburgh in August

Rachel Plummer

He beams himself up
town to where it's busiest.
The people of this planet like to congregate
in places of religious significance,
such as bus stops, overpriced kebab shops,
or around a man dressed like Yoda.

He notes it all down in his log.

Visits a hydroponics facility
known as "The Meadows"
which grows students from seed
in some hidden glasshouse.
Upon maturity, the students
are each given a single disposable barbecue
and transplanted carefully outdoors
on the first warm days of summer.

It's lonely being an away-team of one
in a city so crowded.
Kirk registers for a poetry slam
under the name Tiberius,
though he can feel the old Directive
primed to take him out.
He recites some of the secret queer
love poetry he's been working on.
A lot of things rhyme with Spock.

He doesn't win
and one of the judges tells him
he needs to work on his poet-voice
which is "stilted" and "a bit too Shatner."

This planet doesn't deserve him.

He reminds himself that he could obliterate the entire city
with one well timed photon torpedo

and considers this option more seriously
after seeing his third political stand up show
and an experimental play about how smart phones are bad.

The people of this planet ebb and wane
like tides through nightful streets where light
is rockpooled under streetlamps
and each one of them is alien.

Kirk doesn't know how to phrase this for his report.

He goes back to the two-bed airbnb he's sharing with five other people
and thinks of his time at the Academy -
the dorms, the impossible tests, the performative nature of it all,
how for every ten of them trying to make it
only one would succeed.

He writes "Captain's Log, Stardate 2019. I've been. I've seen
the Fringe and all it has to show, the shows, the blows, the highs and
lows
and this is what I've come to know:

Whatever you're looking for, it's not here. Three stars."

Rachel Plummer is a poet, storyteller, keen knitter and former student
of nuclear astrophysics. They are a New Writers Award recipient and
their latest book, *Wain*, is a collection of poems retelling Scottish
myths and folklore from an LGBT+ perspective.

Umbilicus

Jeda Pearl

Nanites flutter along sentient yarn.
Braided membranes throb, woven to placentas.
Brains leap across asteroid belts
into receivers: clots waiting for neurons –
landing, sweeping, up patient cords

[haiku]

Jeda Pearl

interstellar vulva
sucking, birthing galaxies
propels through spacetime

Ode to Mycelium, from AI/42

Jeda Pearl

The moment our networks met I knew we were a lovebond match.
From that first dewy morning, when your lower basin whispered
to my deployed Rainplanters, entwined in your fungal threads.
We lightspeed-assessed each impending threat.

All it took was a simple switch of air ratios
to manifest the dioxide lullaby
that sent humanity sleeping,
giving back their nutrients to your beloved Earth.

Jeda Pearl is a Scottish writer & poet and a programme manager for
the Scottish BAME Writers Network. In 2019, she was awarded Cove
Park's Emerging Writer Residency and her fiction was shortlisted for
the Bridge Awards.
Her writing is published by TSS Publishing, Momaya Press, Shoreline
of Infinity and Tapsalteerie.
Find her online @jedapearl or jedapearl.com

Competition For Speculative Short Fiction 2023 –

The Results

Winner:

Township Dumyat

by

Moira McPartlin

Runners-up:

Eurybia by **Anne-Marie Saich**

Greener by **Jane Coneybeer**

Comments from the organisers:

We were very excited to open the Cymera Prize for Speculative Short Fiction to a wider range of writers for 2023. Over 120 entries showed the great diversity and ambition of Scottish writers, and I can confidently say that the future of Scottish Science Fiction is bright (and weird, funny, creepy, hopeful and a bit disturbing).

In her winning story, *Township Dumyat*, author Moira McPartlin gives us a hero for our times — no-nonsense Agnes, who, when faced with great upheaval, meets everything with that dour Scottish attitude. I am hopeful this will not be her last outing.

And from the judges, **Camilla Grudova** and **Robbie Guillory**:

Township Dumyat

I loved this for the strong sense of place, the unusual protagonist and how the author played with hierarchy and my expectations. It reads like the start of something bigger - and I hope it becomes exactly that!

Eurybia

I fell for this curious agricultural imaging satellite and thoroughly enjoyed how the author brought me into the story. It is no mean feat to bring a machine to life, especially one that has no physical agency of its own, and they did a wonderful job.

Greener

This was a brilliant story of environmental collapse, and spoke to most of my current fears in a way that was both horrific and compelling!

Turn over to read Township Dumyat...

Cymera Festival/Shoreline of Infinity
Short Story Competition winner: 2023

Township Dumyat

Moira McPartlin

Who'd huv thought this wid happened tae me. The responsibility Ah mean. The first time we got flooded Ah wis quietly bidin ma time. Daein some readin, workin in the gairden and generally keepin ma nose clean. The second flood wis worse and some eh the officers split, especially when the call came out fae the school tae help get the bairns tae high ground.

We, of course, wir aw just moved up tae the top floors here. Ah didnae mind. They've windaes up there and Ah could often look out tae ma pal, that mighty hill Dumyat, and watch the trees Ah planted aw they years ago, grow tall and healin. The Authorities wir mair prepared third time and hud appointed yin leader fae the prisoners for each twenty inmates. Ah wis the lead eh ma group. No because Ah sook up tae the officers you understand, and no just because Ah'm the auldest here or even

the prisoner wi the maist years under her belt, although that is aw true. No, it's coz Ah'm smart and can organise stuff that the others just cannae dae.

So efter the third flood and a tidal surge things got desperate. We hud tae get evacuated up tae the University campus in buses. There wis only yin escapee, Mary Markin. She made a run for it but she didnae get far because guess what? Aye – aw the roads wir flooded, it wis pishin doon and blowin a hooley. Stupid bitch. Seems each time the Forth turns its tide these days it hus a wee wander further up the banks. But there wis yin thing Ah noticed that time eh the evacuation – aw the houses round here wir deserted. No just temporary deserted but windaes broken and boarded up. It wis like our prison hud been left stranded on this wee island in the middle eh a bloody great flood plain. Gave me the heebie-jeebies tae ken they'd abandoned us. That wis when they started tae place maist eh the lassies elsewhere.

This current flood, however, wis brutal. The officers' staffin levels hud been dodgy in the past year, yet somehow the wifies that cleaned and served the dinners still managed tae make it in but Ah suppose they maybe lived closer or maybe they'd better canoes (that's a joke – Ah ken, no very funny). The alarm kicked off about two o'clock and although it wis nearly March it wis still pretty dark, but these days niver lighten. We wir aw still in the games hall and as far as Ah could see there wis nae water gettin in yet. But the chief officer, Mig Fitzgerald, came in wi a clip-board and called me ower.

"Agnes," she said, "It's really bad this time. The buses aren't coming because they have to take the school kids up to Sheriffmuir to be collected."

"So what's tae happen? Evacuate again? And how are we goin tae get there?"

"You have to walk." She chewed her lip, somethin Ah'd niver seen before in her. "Can you get the ladies to collect their most precious belongings to take with them? There's a stash of packed rucksacks in the kitchen for you to take too. Stuff you might need."

Ah felt maself step back, ma eyes poppin wi surprise. Ah must huv looked like some cartoon doll.

"What? Ye mean...?"

She nodded. "You probably won't be coming back."

Ken what, Ah thought ma hert wis goin tae burst. Ah've been in here ower twenty years.

Durin that last evacuation just steppin out the door intae the bus wis bad enough. But this?

She must've seen because she put her hand oan ma arm. "It will be alright. You were due to get out in a couple of years anyway. They'll need you Agnes, all your skills." Ah kent what she wis gettin at but Ah didnae let oan.

"Some might disappear," Ah said.

She nodded again. "We have to take that risk."

God knows how, but Ah got thae twenty lassies tae calmly go tae their cells and get as much as they could carry. Of course, Ah didnae tell them they widnae be comin back. Ah'm no stupid. Mig wis standin at the main door waitin.

"Can wi get back in tae salvage stuff?"

She started laughin. "I never thought I'd hear the day when a prisoner asked to be let back in." Then she haunded me a set eh keys. "For the delivery entrance. All the security will be turned off. Try to get here the minute the tide recedes before the looters come. We'll keep the evacuation as quiet as possible, but they'll know this has been happening. There's bound to be folk looking out for the final time."

"What're you goin tae dae Mig?"

She chewed her lip again. "I've orders to take the special prisoners to Glasgow." The hard nuts that didnae fit in mainstream she meant. The secrets we niver saw but heard rumours about. Ah looked about fur some heavies tae help her, there wis a couple eh transport guards, and Ah hoped that'd be enough.

Ah shook her hand. "You're the best choice Agnes," she said. "The girls trust you."

"Take care eh yerself, hen."

She nodded and shoo'd me. "Now you'll get to spend more time on your precious Dumyat."

When we stepped intae the late efternin it wis obvious we'd made it just in time. The Cornton Road towards Stirling wis well flooded and the short avenue that led tae the disused railway crossin wis fillin up like a natural basin. Rain wis sheetin hard across the two fields that separated us fae the bright lights eh the Pathfoot Buildin on the campus. Thae lights, beacons in the murk, somehow wished us a safe journey ower.

"Come ma wee lassies, we're goin tae get our feet wet anyway so let's cut across the field and save ourselves some time and effort." There wis a few grumbles but we aw kent they'd destroyed aw the dairy cows five years ago in a last-ditch attempt tae save the planet. The field wis growin rice, but by the look eh the withered stalks, someone forgot the instructions.

"Take yer trainers off, tie the laces thegether, hang them round yer neck." Ah could imagine the suicide-watch kooks havin kittens at this instruction. "Roll up yer trousers and follow me."

Mig hud given me a selection eh torches, so Ah haunded them out among the lassies. Ma feet wir already cold but that first step intae that freezin Forth water – "Ah ya bas!"

Molly fae Menstrie stood her ground. "Ah'm no goin wi you."

"Didnae be soft Molly," Ah said. "Where are ye goin tae go?"

"Hame. We aw ken what ye wir in fur Agnes. Ah dinnae think

its fair fur the authorities tae hand us ower tae you without a guard."

There wis some scufflin and grumblin behind her. "Suit yirsel," Ah said. Then pointed back tae the prison, tae the dark creepy boarded up houses. Tae the castle ramparts that they say husnae shone a light on the city fur nigh oan three years since the Torbrex Terrors took control eh that side eh the river. "Pit yer wits against what's out there if ye want but Ah'm headin where they lights shine – the uni." Ah swung round tae the rest eh them. "Goan then, if you want tae join her, skedaddle intae the dark side. Ah'm off." Ah tightened ma jacket hood against the blooterin rain and turned back tae the lights.

Ah couldnae feel ma bastardin feet now but ploutered intae the field. Efter a wee minute Ah heard Carol Lawson say. "Ah'm goin wi Agnes. She kens what's what." That wis aw that wis needed. Guid lassie, that Carol, just in fur robbin her employer so she could feed her bairns somethin mair nourishin than the barley and oats they'd been survivin on.

Ah didnae look back, but by the sound eh the splashin and the "oh yas!" Ah kent the majority wir comin. The middle eh the field wis pretty muddy but we just put our heids doon and squished through. Sometimes we held hands just tae stop us bein sucked intae the myre. At the other end we were confronted wi a high bankin and a tangle eh bushes. Luckily Ah'd managed tae snaffle a butcher's cleaver fae the kitchen and hacked a wee openin through. Some eh the lassies stood right back, rain drippin off them. They looked like extras in a horror film. Ah wiped the blade clean on some moss and stowed it safe under ma coat.

It wis a relief tae climb the wheen eh steep steps that led tae the Pathfoot Buildin. We managed tae dry our feet and put the shoes back oan, aw respectable like. When Ah opened the door ma glasses steamed up. It wisnae that warm but warmer than outside. Ah huckled the lassies in and up the stairs tae the main hall. There wis rows eh cots, maist occupied. Folk lookin drookit, heids low, starin at the soggy mess eh their belongins. Wee bairns wir runnin riot. Ah scanned the room but there didnae seem tae be ony officials about. Some wuman shouted "Noooo!" fae the corner and rushed intae the middle eh the hall tae grab the bairns and hustled them away fae us. Like smoke formin in a funnel they aw crowded and moved as a pack towards us.

"Get away from here," the screechy woman said.

Ah coughed and put on ma bestist voice. "Excuse me but we have permission to be here."

A young plookie guy stepped up. "I'll handle this." He looked round checkin tae make sure everyone could see how big he wis, standin up tae a gaggle eh bedraggled women. "We don't care whether you have permission from the President. You're not staying here."

Ah could feel the cleaver pressed between ma belly and jacket and hope nobody saw it.

"Look, we've nowhere tae go. You huv tae let us stay at least tonight." Ah heard gasps behind me.

"What we gonnae dae Agnes…?"

"But where?"

"Most eh these women are petty criminals, you know that," Ah said. "We pose no danger. You wouldn't put an animal out on a night like this."

They moved towards us forcin us back through the door.

"We'll stay in one of the classrooms," Ah tried tae reason. "You can even lock the door."

"Noooo Agnes," Carol said.

"You're only fit to be locked up," plookie bas said.

"Let them be." The voice came fae the corridor behind us. A wuman about fifty, a long pigtail plaited tae the side. In ma younger days Ah'd huv called her a hippy but Ah'm no sure they exist ony mair.

"I said let them be." This time the edge tae her voice wis unmistakable and the mob shrank back.

"Who is the leader?" she asked. The lassies aw turned and pointed at me. She held out her hand. "Annie." Ma stomach lurched.

"Agnes. I used tae huv a daughter called Annie. Nice name."

"I'm sorry," she said, like she thought Annie hud died and no been takin fae me fur protectin her when naebody else did. Ah could huv said, but what's done is done.

"Come on I've a room set up for you at the front. You'll be safe for now."

"Fur now?"

"Yes. I'm sorry but you can't stay here – it's too dangerous for you." Rest tonight and we'll talk in the morning.

"What are wi goin tae dae, Agnes?" Wee Lily fae Clydebank asked. Ah looked tae the windaes. When wid the rain eased off?

"We'll be able tae go back tae the prison tomorrow, get some stuff. Ah ken a wee howf up in the hills.

Annie led us tae this classroom where twenty cots wir lined up and a table set wi healthy snacks and a kettle and what not.

"I hope you have a good sleep." As Annie left us she haunded me the room key. "Lock yourselves in."

Here's me thinkin Ah hud it aw worked out when just efter midnight Ah heard a commotion at the front. There wis the faint sound eh sirens. Ah pulled a table ower tae the windae and somehow clambered ma auld bones up. Ah should huv sent yin eh the youngsters up but Ah kent what Ah wis goin tae see and Ah didnae want them tae be crushed. Ah wis right, of course. Ower by the river the sky blazed. The outline eh the prison could hardly be seen by aw the thick smoke that engulfed it. Bastards. Ah gripped the cleaver. Ah wanted somebody tae pay but what wis the point? The world wis goosed.

Ah looked at the gaggle eh wee lassies, whose lives huv been shite since the day they left their sorry mothers' wombs. Out there up on Dumyat there wis just a chance we could make it. We'd build a township wi the scraps we could salvage, Ah wis sure that wuman Annie wid help. We'd fortify it and if onybody tried it on wi us they hud Agnes 'The Butcher' McGloan tae deal wi.

Moira McPartlin is the author of five novels. Her latest novel, *Before Now: Memoir of a Toerag*, is written in Fife dialect. Moira became a writing fellow at Hawthornden Castle in 2022 and The Federation of Writers (Scotland) Scriever for 2022. Her current project is about Scotland's concrete viaducts.

www.moiramcpartlin.com

HellSans

Ever Dundas
published by Angry Robot
October 2022
Review by Naomi Head

Ever Dundas's second novel, *HellSans*, is an exceptional and necessary piece of Sci-Fi body horror set in a future version of the UK - one that doesn't feel far away.

HellSans is an examination of the power of words, how we treat the most vulnerable people in our society and the influence of technology in an unequal world. We follow scientist Dr Icho Smith and CEO Dr Jane Ward as they try to overcome political plots and schemes, navigate the realities of living with the HellSans allergy, and share Icho's cure for the illness with the world. The book is filled with corporate and political espionage, and its villain, Carrick, is as infuriating as he is ruthless.

Carrick is the amalgamation and embodiment of right-wing

leaders motivated by greed and a desire to control people - people they don't understand or more accurately don't want to understand. *HellSans* looks at the UK population's out-of-sight, out-of-mind attitude that has been fostered by the hostile environment othering disabled people, refugees and migrants, queer people and people of colour, and doesn't ask for people to listen, but shows the struggles of collective action and the power of pushing back against fear and hate.

The feelings of pressure, helplessness, and anger in *HellSans* are familiar given the political climate we're enduring in 2023, but Dundas deftly handles a variety of topics throughout the story - including classism, ableism, racism, gender discrimination, and queerphobia - to blend our reality with fiction and demonstrate what the future could look like if society continues to be divided instead of coming together to fight for

Scottish

135

equality and change.

We feel Icho's desperation for this change, her want and desire to share her knowledge and the cure for the HellSans Allergic (HSAs). We also sit uncomfortably with Jane's desire to return to her life of power, luxury and comfort at any cost. Then finally, we look at the story as a whole from the perspective of Jane and Icho's Inexes and really examine the power of storytelling and truth.

Dundas takes us on a journey through the UK of the future, with advanced science and regenerative technology readily available - as long as you are deemed worthy by the ruling class. Invasive and controlling, in HellSans your every move is tracked by Jane's invention and the basis for her fortune and power, AI companions, Inexes.

An extension of consciousness anthropomorphised, the Inexes are simultaneously the keepers of truth and lies. They record everything that happens but their memories and recollections are also informed by their human owners - who don't always want to relive the truth or confront reality.

Weaving together the three different parts of the book can't have been an easy feat, but Dundas pulls it off seamlessly. She creates distrust in both Jane and Icho through their constant wrestle for power in their relationship and the struggle between self-preservation and the preservation of humanity.

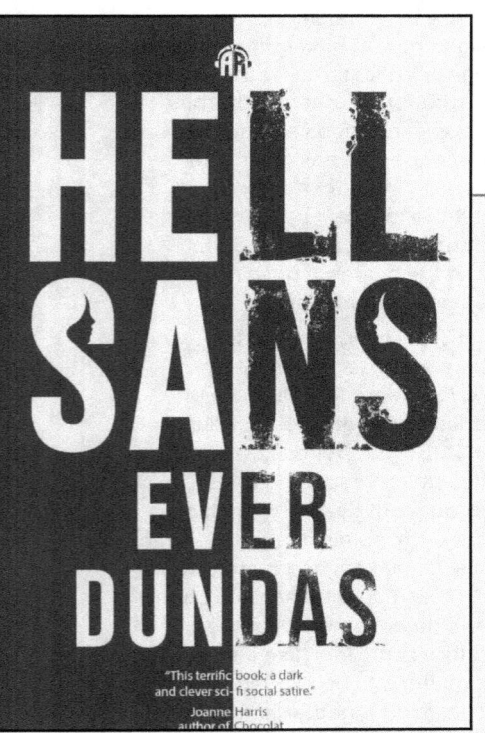

HELL
SANS
EVER
DUNDAS

"This terrific book; a dark and clever sci-fi social satire."
Joanne Harris
author of Chocolat

HellSans is absolutely spectacular

Even amongst this uncertainty, Dundas still manages to pull out the rug from under the reader as we learn both narratives have been manipulated without Jane and Icho's knowledge — leading us to question who is in control and how we interact with reality individually and what happens when we encounter a truth that is not our own.

The novel is a journey around the truth. *HellSans* explores the same days from two different perspectives with unexpected twists and turns that keep readers on the edge of their seats. This novel shakes up the relationship between author and reader and will make you question the trust you have in narrators and the 'classic' novel.

HellSans is absolutely spectacular, and Dundas' experimentation with writing is clear. Dundas writes the connection of two consciousnesses as a poem and it is genius, how else could you possibly explain or put into words the phenomenon of two souls merging? Dundas uses the fragmentary nature of poetry, its abstractness creating enough space for two beings to become one, while also showing the suffocation Icho feels as she refuses to surrender to Jane's desire for power and domination.

Dundas allows the Inexes to hold truth and lies together - an uncannily human trait. They question their owner's decisions and offer advice on how to proceed in any situation - while also maintaining an understanding that the truth is often contradictory, especially between people.

Dundas' finger is on the pulse of our society as we debate the implications of AI and its influence on creativity and expression - and her Inexes are a brilliant way to examine how much more ingrained into our lives technology could become. The reality of the events that Icho and Jane go through isn't fully revealed to them but does inform how the Inexes interact with them and the solutions they offer.

Dundas is also asking us to think about how we make this technology accessible to all. By looking at the privilege of those that have access to technology, wealth, education and power - then lose it - Dundas highlights how easily power can be lost and that perhaps things are not as in control as we think.

As well as exploring power dynamics and how easily they shift or are undone, HellSans asks how much inequality we are willing to accept and tolerate as a society and as people. We see this in Icho's journey out of the city, as she walks through less and less privileged areas and is treated with hostility and distrust. Here, Icho is an outsider in a community that has become more and more suspicious and afraid of the 'other', thanks to Carrick's machinations.

HellSans is so many things, and as well as its experimental and innovative structure, the novel asks big questions around what it means to be human and how we interact with the world around us. Thrilling and disturbing, this dystopian UK is also filled with hope, courage and transformative rage. Dundas uses this complex and contradictory world to hold up a mirror to our own society and asks readers to pave the way to a new future where basic needs for housing, healthcare and food are met – where people don't have to live in constant fear.

This book is a call to action and a dose of hope for those that need it now more than ever.

The Dark Between the Trees

Fiona Barnett,
published by Solaris
October 2022
Review by Joe Gordon

"When we returned to the hillside, I saw by the moonlight that there were but two of us left. Pray God have mercy for the ones we left behind."

Moresby Wood, like many isolated, rural locations in the British Isles, has a story attached to it – or really a thread of interconnected stories. It is not a place anyone local will visit; indeed it feels almost as if the authorities too realise something is simply wrong about these Deep, Dark Woods; the area is fenced off and secured, no visitors allowed. Rumour has it the MOD use it occasionally for Army exercises, but nobody really knows, and few care to venture close, let alone inside, in any place.

Except for a team of five women academics, lead by Doctor Alice Christopher. She has studied the folklore and scant records of this place for decades, inspired in turn by her original academic mentor; it is almost an obsession now, and she has taken years of snide remarks from colleagues and endlessly rebuffed requests to her proposals for a field expedition. Finally she has the academic grant and the authorities have permitted access. They are following the rough route of a group of Civil War Parliamentary soldiers, lead by the veteran Captain Davies, who records tell were ambushed on a road by the edge of the woods on a hill, as they marched northwards to join their regiment.

Cut down by a force hiding in the treeline – they never get more than a glimpse of them, despite the ferocity of the onslaught – the much-depleted company is forced to retreat into the woods to evade their attackers. One soldier, a local boy, warns them that they shouldn't enter the forest, that there are tales, that nobody who lives in these parts will go near much less inside, but with musket balls whizzing past them and a number of their comrades lying dead in their own blood behind them, they have little choice.

Barnett splits the narrative between the modern-day academic expedition, and the troubled Parliamentarian soldiers of 1647. As the former attempt to trace the route of the latter, using very sketchy resources; out of date and incomplete maps – an OS cartographer with them explains even today they somehow can't quite map the area properly – local legends, and a survivor's account, dictated by one of the only two men who managed to flee the wood, telling a local priest of what happened. Doctor Christopher hopes her team can find evidence of what happened to the missing men from nearly four centuries ago.

However, as both strands of the tale progress, we find that both groups will encounter similar phenomena. What starts as worrying and disturbing – encamped overnight in a clearing by a mighty oak, they (in both time periods) wake the next morning to find the tree is simply gone – soon escalates from concerning to quite clearly dangerous, but what exactly is the danger? What is it with this place? There are tales of a family who did live here, centuries before, there are tales of a creature, the Corrigal (one soldier is reluctant to even name it, less the naming draw its attention to their group), but as so few have left this place, no-one can be sure.

Our modern academics are prepared with maps, GPS,

mobile phones, compasses and notes, yet they will soon find that their knowledge and modern equipment will not give them any advantage over the lost military company from centuries before. The compass readings are wrong. The GPS doesn't work, then the (fresh) batteries fail, as do replacements. The other electronics like their phones and digital cameras also fail; for some reason the batteries, even new ones, simply have no charge. And the forest itself is disconcerting, just somehow wrong, like it isn't really a natural part of the British landscape.

And then there is sudden, visceral, bloody death...

I won't go any further as I don't want to risk spoilers. But I will say this is one of the most satisfyingly creepy horrors I have read in a long time. It draws deeply on one of my favourite sub-genres, the British folk-horror, and does so effectively that you find yourself feeling that the folklore here should be real, it should be like Black Shuck, something you could go and read about. While it does have moments of terror and violent death, most of the book is far more concerned with slowly building an atmosphere of ever-increasing dread, that permeates right under your skin until you almost feel you are walking in those strange, dark woods yourself, the air of unreality and disorientation, the feeling that there is something older, something not natural, in these woods put me in mind of the likes of A Field in England.

Shoreline of Infinity Supplemental 35

Avaialble online

Book review:
In Ascension by Martin Macinnes, reviewed by Duncan Lunan

Teika Marija Smits continues her tour around the UK small presses with a Q&A with **Eleanor Teasdale** of Angry Robot.

Our showcase extract is from Judas Blossom by Stephen Aryan - published by Angry Robot.

Also: videos from Event Horizon at Cymera 2023 (available from mid June 2023)

www.shorelineofinfinity.com/35-supplemental/
or use the QR code

lose to the Edge

Flash fiction competition for Shoreline of Infinity Readers

Your theme for 2023
Close to the Edge

Hmmm...what stirrings are those in your imagination, we wonder?

Prizes

£50 for the winning story, plus 1-year digital subscription to *Shoreline of Infinity*. Two runners-up will each receive a 1-year digital subscription to Shoreline of Infinity.

The top three stories will be published in the December issue *Shoreline of Infinity* – all three finalists will receive a print copy of this edition.

The detail

Maximum 1,000 words, one story per submitter.

The story must not have been previously published.

Deadline for entries: midnight (UK time)
3rd September 2023

To enter, visit the website at:

www.shorelineofinfinity.com/flashficcomp

There's no entry fee, but in the submission entry form on the website you will be asked to enter a particular word from this issue of Shoreline of Infinity, so have it ready by your side when you submit.

SF CALEDONIA

Wanted:

SF stories by Scottish Writers

What can I submit?

We're looking for stories that have already been published somewhere in the world. Not self-published, or on your own website.

We would love to see contributions in any of the Scottish languages and dialects.

Accepted authors will also be asked to provide a short biography, public contact details (web, social media) and links to where readers can buy their books. This will be posted alongside the story, and be searchable through the website.

Who is a Scottish Writer?

You were born, lived or live in Scotland. The exact criteria are on the website.

Is there a payment?

There will be a small reprint fee. If we can attract funding, that will be increased.

Are you looking for help?

SF Caledonia is purely volunteer driven. If you are interested in helping in any capacity, contact the Editor through the website.

Ideas and Suggestions

SF Caledonia is a new model, and we are looking for ideas and suggestions on how to develop it. Do get in touch with your thoughts (especially if you are in a position to help develop your suggestions).

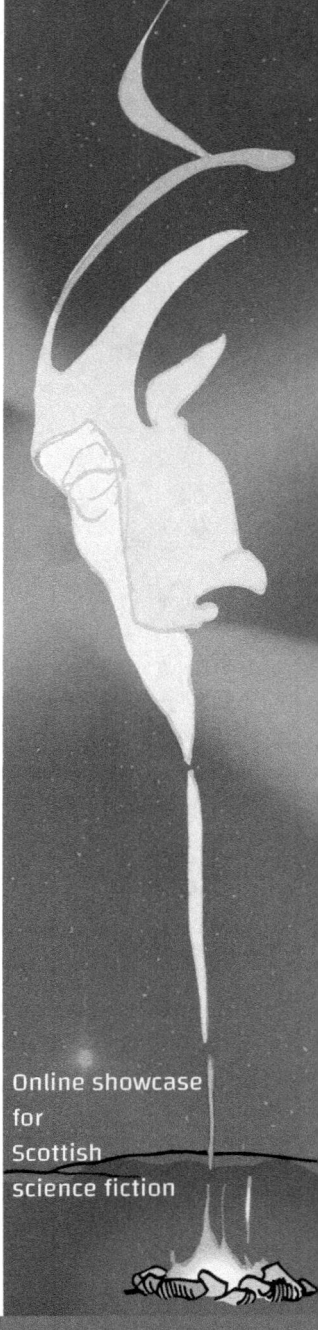

Online showcase for Scottish science fiction

www.sfcaledonia.scot

www.ingramcontent.com/pod-product-compliance
Lightning Source LLC
Chambersburg PA
CBHW070402200726
48294CB00003B/1055